"She wants what?" Patrick Larson said in consternation a month later.

"She wants us to acquire an ocean-going vessel that will transport horses, people, and household goods. She has decided to go to Australia to claim her inheritance. Apparently, she has sold her family ranch in the valley to a relative, who we have obtained as a client. He has written us too, asking about the impending legal fight for the ranch. She writes to us asking that we obtain passage for her, her children, a few cousins, and her herd of horses," Simon said as though she had lost her mind.

Patrick looked at Simon as though he was the one who had lost his mind and not their client, Carmen.

"Don't shoot the messenger," Simon dared to say. Patrick smiled sardonically. That was exactly how he was feeling. Carmen hadn't given up the fight. It would continue with the relative, who had bought her ranch. She was going to start anew in Australia. What a brave soul!

A K'Anne Meinel novella

Novels in Paperback:

SHIPS *CompanionSHIP, FriendSHIP,*
RelationSHIP
Long Distance Romance
Children of Another Mother
Erotica
The Claim
Bikini's Are Dangerous
The Complete Series
Germanic
Malice Masterpieces 1
The First Five Books
Represented
Timed Romance
Malice Masterpieces 2
Books Six through Ten
The Journey Home
Out at the Inn
Shorts
Anthology Volume 1
Lawyered
Malice Masterpieces 3
Books Eleven through Fifteen
Blown Away

Blown Away
The Alternate Cover
Small Town Angel
Pirated Love
Doctored
Veil of Silence
Malice Masterpieces 4
Books Sixteen through Twenty
The Outsider
Pirated Heart
Recombinant Love
Survivors
Inn the Dog House
Flight
An Island Between Us

Vetted Series:
Vetted
Cavalcade (Prequel)
Pioneering (Prequel)
Vetted Further
Vetted Again

Novellas in Paperback:

Mysterious Malice (Book 1)
Meticulous Malice (Book 2)
Mistaken Malice (Book 3)
Malicious Malice (Book 4)
Masterful Malice (Book 5)
Matrimonial Malice (Book 6)
Mourning Malice (Book 7)
Murderous Malice (Book 8)
Mental Malice (Book 9)
Menacing Malice (Book 10)
Minor Malice (Book 11)
Morally Malice (Book 12)
Morose Malice (Book 13)
Melancholy Malice (Book 14)
Mad Malice (Book 15)
Macabre Malice (Book 16)
Marinating Malice (Book 17)

Macerating Malice (Book 18)
Minacious Malice (Book 19)
Meddlesome Malice (Book 20)
Meandering Malice (Book 21)
Vaquera Safica (Spanish)
Surfista Safica (Spanish)
ケーアンヌ・マイネル (Japanese)
Maniacal Malice (Book 22)
Sayyida
The Northwood Lodge
Monitoring Malice (Book 23)
Marked Malice (Book 24)
Shanghaied
Outback Born
Outback Bred

Pocket Paperbacks:

Mysterious Malice (Book 1)
Sapphic Surfer
Sapphic Cowgirl
Meticulous Malice (Book 2)
Mistaken Malice (Book 3)
Malicious Malice (Book 4)
Masterful Malice (Book 5)
Matrimonial Malice (Book 6)
Mourning Malice (Book 7)
Murderous Malice (Book 8)
Mental Malice (Book 9)
Menacing Malice (Book 10)
Minor Malice (Book 11)
Morally Malice (Book 12)
Morose Malice (Book 13)
Melancholy Malice (Book 14)
Mad Malice (Book 15)
Macabre Malice (Book 16)
Marinating Malice (Book 17)

In E-Book Format:
Short Stories

Fantasy
Wet & Wet Again
Family Night
Quickie ~ Against the Car
Quickie ~ Against the Wall
Quickie ~ Over the Couch
Mile High Club
Quickie ~ Under the Pier
Heel or Heal
Kiss
Family Night 2
Beach Dreams
Internet Dreamers
Snoggered
On the Parkway
Stable Affair
Kept
Stolen
Agitated
Love of my LIFE
Quickie in an Elevator,
GOING DOWN?
Into the Garden
The Book Case
The Other Women
Menage a WHAT?

E-Book Novellas

Children of Another Mother
Bikini's are Dangerous
Ghostly Love
Bikini's are Dangerous 2
Sapphic Surfer
The Rockhound
Bikini's are Dangerous 3
Bikini's are Dangerous 4
Bikini's are Dangerous 5
Mysterious Malice (Book 1)
Meticulous Malice (Book 2)
Mistaken Malice (Book 3)
Malicious Malice (Book 4)
Masterful Malice (Book 5)
Matrimonial Malice (Book 6)
Mourning Malice (Book 7)
Murderous Malice (Book 8)
Sapphic Cowgirl
Sapphic Cowboi
Mental Malice (Book 9)
Menacing Malice (Book 10)
Charming Thief
~Snake Island~
Charming Thief
~Diamonds are a Girls Best Friend~
Minor Malice (Book 11)
Morally Malice (Book 12)
Morose Malice (Book 13)
Melancholy Malice (Book 14)
Mad Malice (Book 15)
Macabre Malice (Book 16)
Marinating Malice (Book 17)
Macerating Malice (Book 18)
Minacious Malice (Book 19)
Sayyida
Meddlesome Malice (Book 20)
Meandering Malice (Book 21)
Maniacal Malice (Book 22)
The Northwood Lodge
Monitoring Malice (Book 23)
Marked Malice (Book 24)
Shanghaied
Outback Born
Outback Bred

E-Book Novels

SHIPS *CompanionSHIP, FriendSHIP, RelationSHIP*
Erotica Volume 1
Long Distance Romance
Bikini's Are Dangerous
The Complete Series
Malice Masterpieces
The First Five Books
To Love a Shooting Star
Germanic
The Claim
Represented
Timed Romance
Blown Away
Blown Away *The Alternate Cover*
Malice Masterpieces 2
Books Six through Ten
The Journey Home
Out at the Inn
Anthology Volume 1
Lawyered

Malice Masterpieces 3
Books Eleven through Fifteen
Small Town Angel
Pirated Love
Doctored
Veil of Silence
Malice Masterpieces 4
Books Sixteen through Twenty
The Outsider
Pirated Heart
Recombinant Love
Survivors
Inn the Dog House
Flight
An Island Between Us

Vetted Series:
Vetted
Cavalcade (Prequel)
Pioneering (Prequel)
Vetted Further
Vetted Again

LARGE Print Novels

SHIPS CompanionSHIP, FriendSHIP, RelationSHIP
Erotica Volume 1
Long Distance Romance
Children of Another Mother
Bikini's Are Dangerous
The Complete Series

Malice Masterpieces
The First Five Books
To Love a Shooting Star
The Claim
Represented
Timed Romance

Audiobooks

Doctored
Sapphic Surfer
The Rockhound
Cavalcade

Pioneering
To Love A Shooting Star
Mysterious Malice

Videos

Biography of Books
Ships
Sapphic Surfer
Ghostly Love
Long Distance Romance
Germanic
Sensual Sapphic
Sapphic Cowgirl
Couples
Lie Next To Me

Sapphic Cowboi
Timed Romance
Readings (SHIPS)
Doctored
Veil of Silence
She's Coming (The Outsider short)
It's Coming (The Outsider short)
The Outsider
Vetted

K'ANNE MEINEL

ISBN-13: 978-1733661164

K'Anne Meinel is available for comments at KAnneMeinel@aim.com as well as on Facebook @ http://www.facebook.com/K.Anne.Meinel.Fan.Page, Google + @ https://plus.google.com/u/2/+KAnneMeinel, LinkedIn @ https://www.linkedin.com/in/k-anne-meinel-a026385a, or her blog @ http://kannemeinel.wordpress.com/ or on Twitter @ https://twitter.com/KAnneMeinel, or on her website @ www.kannemeinel.com if you would like to follow her to find out about stories and book's releases.

www.shadoepublishing.com

ShadoePublishing@gmail.com

Shadoe Publishing, LLC is a United States of America company

Cover by: K'Anne Meinel @ Shadoe Publishing
Edited by: Deb Amia, Grammar Queen grammarqueen.com

**Dedicated to anyone who
thinks I'm writing about them.
I am.**

PUBLISHER'S NOTE
This is a work of fiction. Names, characters, places, and incidents are the product of the author's imagination or are used fictitiously, and any resemblance to actual persons, living or dead, business establishments, events, or locales is entirely coincidental.
The publisher does not have any control over and does not assume any responsibility for author or third-party Web sites or their content.

CHAPTER ONE

"So, you see, Mrs. Pearson, your uncle has bequeathed you half the entire ranch," the big city lawyer told her patiently and a bit condescendingly, almost as though she hadn't understood him the first or second time.

She nodded to show she was listening as she thought over everything he had told her.

"I also have an offer from the cousins here," he indicated a letter on his desk, "to purchase your half," he continued. "I think it's a fair offer and you should take it." He pushed some papers across his desk as he looked at her. "If you'll sign here, I can write them and arrange for payment."

"May I have some time to think about it?" she asked uncertainly.

He was annoyed at the delay but tried to hide it. "What is there to think about, Mrs. Pearson? You've received a *bona fide* offer," he stressed the words as though she were too country to understand them, "for your inheritance, which is half a world away. I advise you to take the offer before they withdraw it."

She nodded thoughtfully. "Well, this is a lot to think about. Uncle Jude wrote to me faithfully, and I'm shocked to learn that he died and all."

He nodded. He was sure she was shocked, although he didn't know a lot about his client. He was handling it under the direction of one of the senior partners, who owed someone in Australia a favor. He wasn't sure this country bumpkin understood exactly what she had inherited. "Why don't you go back to your hotel and think it over? We can have another meeting tomorrow and discuss things while you sign the papers. I'm sure you will have your monies in a few months."

She was aggravated, but he would never have known it. His condescension had begun the moment she entered the office. She had worn her Sunday best for this meeting with the big city lawyer, but it was apparent that her Sunday best didn't measure up to his idea of what women should wear. As she left the offices, she saw what other women in the city were wearing and realized she did look like a country girl dressed up to visit the city for the day. She shook her head. *When had that happened?*

Carmen made her way to a taxi stand and had them drive her back to the Clairmont Hotel. On the way, she asked the driver if he knew a ready-made dressmaker, who might have some clothes she could purchase. He nodded and altered his direction just a few blocks from the Clairmont. She tipped him and thanked him as she made her way into the establishment.

"Yes, may I help you?" a pleasant-faced woman greeted her.

"Hello, I'm Mrs. Pearson. I've come into the city, and as you can see, I'm hopelessly out of date in my fashion." She grinned ruefully as she indicated the dress she was wearing. She warmed when the lady smiled encouragingly, not in derision or condescension. "I've been told you have ready-made dresses?"

"You've been told correctly." She smiled again, pleased that someone had referred this woman to her shop. "I have a few things that will look marvelous on you with your coloring." She began to show Carmen around the shop.

In no time at all, and with only a few minor alterations, Carmen had two new dresses. She would donate her old dress to a charity later. On second thought, maybe she would keep it. One never knew when they might need an old dress. She felt elegant, sophisticated, and like a townie in her new outfit as she made her way back to the Clairmont Hotel. No one accosted her, and she was grateful that she didn't need to use the pistol she kept in her bag. She looked confident and her stride showed that. She drew many admiring glances as she made her way back to her hotel. At the desk she asked for directions to the city's public library, and she was pleased that it was within walking distance of the hotel. She spent her afternoon very productively.

"Mrs. Pearson?" the lawyer gasped in astonishment at the change in her appearance in only one day.

"Good morning," she responded. She felt one hundred percent better now that she'd had a chance to think about the repercussions of what Uncle Jude had left her. She felt more confident after studying up on Australia and the Outback where her uncle's ranch was located. She had located what little information was available at the library, although precious little had been written, just a few newspaper articles and books. She had learned they didn't call them ranches though, they called them stations. She looked forward to re-reading her uncle's letters to refresh her memory of everything he had ever told her about his lifestyle in Australia.

"I have the papers right here, if you'd care to sign," he pushed them across the desk towards her, holding out a quill pen for her to sign with, the ink bottle to her right.

"I don't think so, Mr. Wainwright. I've decided to keep my share of the station…" She saw his look of consternation before she added, "for now. In fact, I would like you to inquire as to the value of the station, its productivity level, and other such information on my behalf."

"As I stated yesterday, you have a bona fide offer from your cousins–" he began again, but she raised her hand to cut him off.

"Yes, you told me that yesterday. Uncle Jude's heirs…my cousins…I get that. We own the ranch, er, station together, and they wish to buy me out. I require more information before making such an important decision. You say their offer is fair but what exactly is fair? Values of land in Australia are as precarious as our western lands here in America. I want to be certain I have full knowledge of things before I make a decision."

"I'm sure you do, but I assure you–" he began in a superior tone, and again, she cut him off.

"Are you working as attorney for my cousins, or are you working as my attorney and on my behalf?" she pinned him with her gaze. Yesterday, she had been stunned to learn Uncle Jude had left her his half of the station. Perhaps overwhelmed better described how she was feeling, hence the reason for her visit to San Francisco. Today, she was more confident, and she wasn't going to be steamrolled into a decision based on *this* man's advice.

"Neither." He shook his head angrily at her question. "I am working for one of the senior partners, who was contacted by an attorney in Sydney on your cousins' behalf. As you know, half the ranch is owned outright by both cousins, who received their father's share of the ranch. You, as your uncle's heir, now own his half of the ranch."

"Since they are obviously running the entire station at this time and intend to run it until this matter is settled, it shouldn't be difficult to ask a few questions and get me some information," she stated reasonably.

He sighed. What had seemed like a simple inheritance matter was turning into a lot of work…work he didn't want or need. "There is the matter of the time it takes for a letter to get across the Pacific and out to the ranch. I understand it is some distance from Sydney."

"You have a point, and my uncle died quite some time ago, well before I was informed. This matter will remain unsettled until my questions are answered to my satisfaction, and I make an informed decision," she informed him forcefully.

He swallowed his ire. The partners weren't going to be happy with this delay. What had seemed simple had suddenly become complicated due to this country bumpkin. Although today, she seemed a totally different woman from the one who had timidly entered his office the previous day.

Carmen gestured at the will and papers on his desk. "May I keep these copies?"

He looked down at the papers, then up at her, surprised by the question. "These are my copies. The others are being kept in the office safe," he informed her indignantly. "Another set should be arriving by mail." Nowadays, it was standard practice to send several copies by mail since ships had been known to go down and mail could easily be lost.

"Then, may I keep these copies?" she asked.

He eyed her suspiciously. "You cannot inherit or sell the station until things are settled here," he tried to inform her.

"I'm not selling anything until I get the information I requested," her eyebrow raised, "and apparently, I've already inherited it, and I just have to decide what to do with it."

He eyed her sharply. She was a lot smarter than he had given her credit for the day before. Perhaps, it had all been an act to throw him off. The thought that she might have somehow tricked him angered him. His abrupt retort was cut off when a knock sounded on his door. Without waiting for his answer, a head popped in. "You about done?" the man asked.

The lawyer stood up from his chair immediately. "I'm finishing up here with Mrs. Pearson," he said by way of excuse, gesturing at the woman sitting before his desk. He gulped self-consciously and straightened his suit.

The man glanced at the woman sitting across the desk from the lawyer and smiled in delight. "Mrs. Pearson?" He came into the room, held out his hand, and she stood up. "I'm Patrick Larson. I knew your father before he passed away. I'm delighted to finally meet you. I am so sorry about your uncle. I never met him personally, but if your father's brother was anything like him, I'm sure he was quite a man!"

Carmen was momentarily overwhelmed by the greeting after the lukewarm attitude of the lawyer assigned to her. "It's a pleasure to meet you, Mr. Larson," she murmured appreciatively.

"Is Simon here taking care of you?" he boomed cordially as he released her hand.

"Well, we were discussing the terms of my uncle's will and whether I should sell the property or–"

"Sell it?" he asked in astonishment. "Do you realize how large the station is?"

She shook her head as she recovered her equilibrium. "That is what Mr. Wainwright and I were discussing. I need a lot more information before I make an informed decision about the property."

"Who has made an offer for the station?" he turned to Simon; his eyes fierce.

Simon swallowed self-consciously. "The cousins..." he began weakly.

Patrick nearly growled as he held out his hand. "Let me see the will and the offer," he demanded.

Simon handed over the papers reluctantly. He knew he was going to catch hell about this now. If she had just signed the paperwork the previous day, everything would be settled, his work would be done, and he would have already moved on to other more important matters.

Carmen looked on in astonishment at the way things had suddenly changed. She waited patiently as Mr. Larson perused the paperwork, his eyes missing nothing as he rapidly scanned the documents. She could see from the corner of her eye that Mr. Wainwright was a little impatient to be standing there as he fidgeted.

Finally, Patrick looked up. "I would advise against accepting this offer for now. I would recommend getting an assessor out there immediately and confirming the value of the property. I know your uncle and his cousin had grazing licenses, but your father mentioned that they were looking into acquiring the land legally. Twin Station is not a small endeavor, and I don't believe this offer is adequate for what it would entail."

Carmen felt relieved. She had been worried about what her own stubbornness would cost her. Simon's superior knowledge made her feel justified in asking for the same information.

"It will take months to get a letter there and months for a reply–" Simon began but halted at the look from Patrick.

"These things always take time. It might take years, especially with the heirs in different countries." He indicated Carmen. Turning to her, he asked, "Do you have the time to wait, Mrs. Pearson?"

She smiled and nodded. "Yes, but I have to get back to the valley. I only intended to be in the city for a few days, and those days are now up," she said regretfully.

"Ah, the next time you are in the city, you must allow me to buy you dinner. I would enjoy it." He turned to Simon, "You'll draft the necessary paperwork in quadruplicate?"

"Quadruplicate, sir?" Simon asked, unsure.

"Yes. Two copies will be mailed to Australia on separate ships to ensure that one reaches its destination, one for our files, and one copy for Mrs. Pearson, of course," he said in a tone that implied Simon should have known better.

"Of course, sir," Simon hastily assured him. "I'll do that immediately. You will have your copy this afternoon, Mrs. Pearson. I'll have it messengered to your hotel."

Carmen smiled and gathered the papers Mr. Larson handed her; she had the desired copies now. "I'll be leaving by stage first thing in the morning. See that you arrange that," she answered Mr. Wainwright with a smile.

"Allow me to escort you out, Mrs. Pearson," Patrick offered gallantly.

Simon heaved a sigh of relief when they both left and immediately began writing a draft of the letter that must be sent to Australia. He realized that he might have just angered a senior partner by pressuring Mrs. Pearson into settling the estate too quickly, but he had only wanted to clear the matter up promptly. He hoped his industriousness would impress Mr. Larson and he wouldn't be angry, possibly costing Patrick his position with the firm. It was obvious Mr. Larson valued Mrs. Pearson's patronage.

CHAPTER TWO

Carmen took the mid-morning stage the next day as she had planned. She was wearing the second of her new dresses, her bag on top of the stage containing the rest of her wardrobe. She had read over the paperwork many times; the terms of her uncle's will clear to her now despite the legal wording of it all. The property known as Twin Station was left jointly to her and her two cousins. Originally, two brothers had owned it, and they each had children. One had a son, and the other had two sons. The one with two sons had sent the younger son out into the world with an education and enough money to start his own station, but instead, he had immigrated to America and met a local woman whose family had a ranch that he helped to develop. That man had been Carmen's father, and that ranch was now Carmen's. The other uncle/cousin with only one son had two heirs, the brother and sister, who had offered to purchase Carmen's share in the station. The money was good, but Carmen suspected it might be less than the actual value of the station, and she wanted more information. The little she had learned about Australia from the city library had told of a wonderous new land, but apparently, not a lot was known about it yet. The interior was basically unexplored, and it amazed her that a huge bit of land like Australia was still relatively unknown.

Originally a penal colony, Australia had slowly welcomed free settlers, who availed themselves of the labors of those incarcerated for various crimes. Some of those convicts worked off their period of incarceration until they were free and, depending on their crimes, they returned to England. Some stayed and became members of the growing communities in Australia. At first, the Blue Mountains kept them away from the interior. The strange animals, the bugs, and the aboriginal people were all very different from what anyone had seen before. Expansion was slow as farming and ranching was different from what people had known in England, but people adapted as they learned. Selections or small farms were the norm, but as the land was vast and seemingly unlimited, larger ranches or stations began to develop. Sheep and cattle began to be bred in numbers that staggered the imagination. People from all over the world began to migrate to this new and diverse land.

Carmen returned to her own ranch in the Central Valley with mixed emotions. She had watched her father build up the ranch after marrying a Spanish-Mexican's daughter, who brought him respectability in the valley that was mostly controlled by Dons. The Dons were slowly losing their heritage to the Americans that arrived in droves to California and discovered the lush and fertile valley. She had grown up here, married here, and been widowed here. Among the vast fields of grain, the huge orchards of fruits, and the hillsides full of cattle, were a lot of drifting men who came to California to find their fortunes when gold was discovered in its mountains and streams, but they found it wasn't as easy to thrive here as they had been led to believe. Thefts of food, cattle, and other things were common, and Carmen was grateful when her stage was met by some of her own men, many distant cousins of her mother's.

"Ola, Senora Carmen. How was your trip to the city?" A nattily dressed man with dark black hair, a huge sombrero, and black moustache grinned to her from his horse as he held another for her.

"It was interesting, Paco." She smiled at him as he jumped down, handing her the reins to the horse he was leading. She smiled up at the big, black horse, who immediately began nuzzling against her as she patted it affectionately.

"He doesn't act that way with anyone else," the man mumbled resentfully as he took her bag to fasten it to the back of his saddle.

"That's because he loves me, and he merely tolerates everyone else," she said laughingly as she walked to the horse's side where Paco helped her to scramble into the side saddle.

"A side saddle?" she murmured to him quietly.

"I thought this once you might like to look like a lady," he answered saucily.

"You thought right," she indicated the fine dress she was wearing, clearly not riding attire, and she grinned in return. She looped her knee over the saddle to hold herself on the back of her stallion and adjusted her skirts.

Side saddle or astride, she was a good rider, and they were soon on their way. They rode rapidly away from the town, spectators watching as she effortlessly controlled the big stallion. Two more riders following behind grinned happily as Carmen greeted them.

"Any problems while I was away?" she asked Paco, who rode next to her with his hand near his pistol, always alert.

He shrugged. "What are problems these days?" he hedged in answer.

She sighed. She knew what the problems were. They were the same they had always been there in her father's time and in her grandfather's time. Her father hadn't had the same prejudices to deal with from the whites streaming into the state but her grandfather and cousins had. Her father had to deal with the Mexicans because he was one of those hated gringos. Her mother had loved him, and he had not only loved her in return but adored and worshipped her. He had been nearly devastated when she died giving birth to a little boy, who hadn't survived much beyond his mother. In her absence, he had heaped his affections on their only daughter and heir, his letters to his brother and cousins proudly telling of their niece and cousin and her accomplishments. As a result, his brother had left his only heir and niece his half of the station in Australia. He could have left it all to his cousins who lived there but he hadn't. Carmen wondered at that. Why hadn't he left it to the cousins? They knew the Outback, and they knew the station. She lived in America and knew nothing about running a sheep station.

She also knew in all probability that her father had confided in his family about all the problems they had encountered on their own ranch here in the Central Valley. Drifters, con-artists, and bureaucrats were constantly trying to put aside the old land grants that the Mexicans had had for hundreds of years, long before these others had moved into the rich state of California. Their own ranch was relatively small, yet solvent because her father had been white and her grandfather was a Don, but still, people coveted the rich land. After the death of first, her father and then, her weak husband, Carmen was alone. She had her four children to raise, and she would do this as she saw fit. She had received many offers for their little ranch, but she had held out for two years now despite the pressures mounting exorbitantly. Slowly, her cattle had been stolen. She had tracked down the thieves numerous times and hung them as a warning to others, and still, others came to try again. But her horses were her babies, and they were jealously guarded. A new kind of horse and cattle thief had come into the valley, and she knew it was only a matter of time until they outmaneuvered her. She had meant to ask the city attorney, perhaps she would write to him…not that Mr. Wainwright but Mr. Larson.

When she returned to the hacienda, Carmen learned that someone had run off with several heads of cattle and three of her prized horses. They had caught up with both thieves, but their heads had been blown away before her men could hang them. "I think someone is trying to impress you," Paco informed her.

Carmen had been courted often during her two years of widowhood but found no one who excited her. She had married a man too weak to protect her. She had been too young to realize there were things more important than looks. Still, he had given her beautiful children, his good looks and her Hispanic and European heritage coming through in the children. His death had been a relief. She had mourned him properly, but she intended to marry for love next time, if there was a next time.

"Mama, Mama, Mama," three voices yelled in chorus as she pulled up and slid from her saddle. After ground tying her horse, she opened her arms and the children ran into them. Three little boys hugged her exuberantly as a Mexican woman came out with a little girl in her arms.

After giving the boys each a hug and a squeeze, she reached for the little girl. "Mama," the small girl said shyly as she smiled endearingly, a dimple on each cheek.

"Rachel, my darling. How are you?" Carmen asked the little girl, who held her close.

"Mama, can we go ride?" asked the oldest of the three little boys.

"Why don't you take Dancer to the barn and unsaddle him," she responded. The boys lit up at the importance of the job. Not everyone could handle Dancer, but the stallion allowed them to pull him along to the barn, strangely docile in the presence of the little boys.

"You know that horse is a killer?" Paco mentioned quietly as he watched the children heading to the barn.

Carmen laughed with genuine humor and said, "Then you better hurry up," as she carried her daughter into the house.

CHAPTER THREE

Carmen wrote her letter to the attorney in San Francisco. She didn't believe in procrastinating. She was kicking herself. She had just been there, and she could have asked his advice on the ranch and the problems they had been having.

She was so very tired. She had washed up before dinner. The welcome food had filled her, but the trip had exhausted her. Dealing with the problems on the ranch was slowly eroding her confidence. She had plenty of help, mostly from cousins and other relatives who lived in the vicinity, but she knew it was only a matter of time before the thieves stole what was rightfully hers. After writing her letter, she asked one of the boys that worked on the ranch to take it into town and mail it when he went for supplies tomorrow.

Over the next few days, the sophisticated clothes she had bought in San Francisco were tucked away in favor of a split skirt, knee-high boots, and a corduroy shirt that she tucked in with a belt sporting a pretty powerful looking gun hanging from it. Carmen worked her ranch as much as any owner in the valley. She supervised the workers that lived there and the migrant workers that came and went with the seasons. She worked her own horses, her babies, after having started a breeding program that was the envy of many horse lovers. That was why her horses were frequently the target of thieves as well as buyers. She had started with a thoroughbred mustang cross, then introduced a Hanoverian Belgian cross, and as a result, the horses she had were tall, muscular, and hardy. They could ride all day, pull heavy loads, and still were beautiful. She only sold horses that didn't live up to her high standards. The two dozen adults she had left, some with foals, some still pregnant, were part of her breeding program. They were expensive, but they were still her babies. She kept a watchful eye on them. Dancer was father to many of them. He had been the firstborn of the original crosses, and he was a beautiful example of good, selective breeding. He was also very dangerous. He had killed several people, who had made attempts to steal him or part of his harem. He was strangely gentle to Carmen and her children though. He tolerated Paco and a couple of the handlers, but anyone else was in danger from the large, midnight-blue-colored stallion. His coal black eyes penetrated with an icy chill, but his beauty left you breathless. His offspring were every bit as beautiful as he was, but none were as mean.

Carmen rode Dancer around the ranch in the following weeks, inspecting and prying into every aspect of her operation. Dancer protected her and got her where she needed to go…fast. Nothing felt better than giving him his head and allowing him to take her where he would, rapidly crossing the miles of ranchland. She loved this land she had been born to, and yet, she was coming to resent it. It had killed her father, her husband, and indirectly, her mother and grandfather. She was tired of the strife, and she was tired of the battle. She owned and worked this land—it was hers by right of inheritance—but still, she had to fight for it more often than she liked. She looked at the acres of tilled land, the orchards, and the animals in her fields and wondered how long she could hold on. She instinctively knew that the time of large rancheros was coming to an end, and she was curious what would happen to the Dons and their offspring as the Americans came in and tried to take over. There would be bloodshed, of that she was certain.

Weeks after she returned from the city, she received another thinly veiled threat in the form of an offer from another shady businessman in town. She received at least one like this every month, so she simply ignored it. However, when someone began taking shots at her workers and scaring them off, she realized this one was different. The others had merely been nuisances, but it seemed that someone really wanted this ranch, small as it was, and they were determined to get it. She increased the patrols by her cousins and ranch hands but still near misses occurred. She herself went out and *practiced* with her rifle and pistols, nearly hitting a trespasser once. The near misses stopped for a time after that, but she began to think she might have to order her people to shoot all trespassers on sight, and that couldn't be allowed. If they shot a trespasser, the law wouldn't help her. She was aware that the Anglos made the laws to favor themselves, not the Hispanics, who had lived here for hundreds of years.

She received a reply from Mr. Larson about looking into the problems of their valley. He expressed his condolences and promised to have friends in high places investigate the matter. When no further incidents had occurred for a while, she wasn't sure if the harassment she had been receiving ended because of her shooting back or because of Mr. Larson's influence, but she was very grateful it had stopped. Her lawyer went on to say they hadn't heard from Australia yet, but they would let her know as soon as they did. She had known their inquires would take months, even years, with the distance a letter had to travel.

The fruit crops were all in and sent to town when Paco came back with an odd sight. Mr. Larson was following on one of their spare horses looking awkward mounted on the horse in his San Francisco suit.

"Why, Mr. Larson," Carmen said, astonished to see him. "This is a delightful surprise," she told him. "Why didn't you use a buggy?" she asked as she helped steady him once he slid off the horse.

"Sheer pride," he said disgustedly. "I thought I'd be like this young buck here," he indicated Paco with his thumb, who was grinning unrepentedly as he gathered the reins and turned back to the barn. The wagons of supplies made their way into the covered sheds. "Apparently, my body is not as agile as my mind." He straightened slowly, grateful for her steadying hand on his arm.

"Well, come in and put your feet up. Dinner is almost on the table. You'll join us for a few days, won't you?" Carmen offered.

"Yes, my dear, I will. Thank you. I was hoping you'd ask. I've always been curious about the ranch your father inherited…from your maternal grandfather, wasn't it?" he asked as they made their way up the stairs.

"Yes, my pappy had a land grant that was confirmed when California became part of the United States. My father's marriage to his daughter allowed a gringo into their sacred halls," she joked, knowing the prejudices worked both ways between Mexicans and whites.

"So you said in your letter," Patrick Larson replied as she led him into a cool room in the front of the large ranch house. He sat in a well-upholstered leather chair gratefully.

"Can I get you a drink before dinner?" she offered.

He accepted gratefully and was surprised by how smooth the gin tasted. "This is wonderful. Where did you buy it?"

"We have our own still. It's a family recipe." She grinned as she sipped her own glass.

He shook his head. "Totally self-sufficient out here, aren't you?" He smiled as he took another delightful taste.

"You didn't come all the way out here to drink our gin, did you?" she teased. She had to admit she was surprised to see the powerful attorney all the way out here in the valley.

He grinned. "Get right to the point, eh? That's fine," he took another sip. "You wouldn't happen to make whiskey too, would you?"

She laughed and rose to take his now empty gin glass and pour a bit of the darker alcohol for him. "No, I don't make whiskey, but this should take care of the few aches and pains you might have."

He took a sip and sighed appreciatively. The whiskey was also smooth and tasted excellent. He looked around the sparsely furnished room, noting the few pieces in it were comfortable and functional. The

chair he found himself in invited the user to sink in and relax. He knew he would fall asleep in it, if he weren't careful. It had been a long trip out to this ranch he had been so curious about. "Are we alone?" he asked in a moderately low voice as he glanced at the archways to the room.

She shrugged. "My children are around somewhere and also their nurses, my cousins, and a few workers, but they won't interrupt, if that's what you are worried about." She looked at him curiously, wondering why he had made this trip from the city.

He glanced around again. "I just don't wish to be overheard. Do you have an office or perhaps a den?"

She nodded and beckoned. They entered the cool hall, the tiles a deep rich red-brown and crossed it to a double-doored room. She opened one side, and he followed her into a richly appointed room, even more richly appointed than the living room they had just left. This room had obviously been a man's study or den, judging by the bull horns on the walls, the furniture upholstered with cowhide in various patterns, and the rich, dark, wood furniture and shelves. She gestured to a couch and took a seat across from him as she looked at him curiously, waiting for him to begin his story of what had brought him to the ranch.

Patrick cleared his throat and took another sip of the whiskey. "Well, let me begin. I investigated the situation here at the ranch, and you do own the title outright. However, there are wheels being set in motion to put aside all land grants for the past one hundred years, and this would include your grandfather's land grant. Your grandfather was a wise man. By marrying his only daughter to your father, a white man, he was assured that the land that had been in his family for generations would be protected. Here is where it gets tricky though. Someone, and I honestly don't know who, wants to take issue with the fact that your father was British and not American. They want to put aside the land grant based on that." He held up a hand to keep Carmen from interrupting before he finished. "It's going to be an expensive legal battle for you. As far as I'm concerned, you would win, but it might begger you, which is what someone might be counting on. You are a natural-born American citizen, but you are a woman, and they will try every dirty trick they can to do you out of what is rightfully yours. Again, you would win with me representing you, but at what cost?" He looked at her sorrowfully. She was pretty with her black eyes and long, curly, brown hair that was so dark it was almost black. The dark good looks inherited from her mother combined with her Anglo father's looks had produced a very pretty woman.

"You're saying I have to prove I own my own land?" she asked, incredulously.

He nodded. "Essentially, that is what it boils down to. These men are determined. They don't believe the Mexicans should have any say in this land. They believe the land is American, even if the Mexicans were here hundreds of years before the whites. I will fight for you, and I will win, but they will use every underhanded trick they can think of, if they haven't already."

She thought about the potshots, the near misses, and the thefts. She had thought these were random and separate acts, but they might all be part of someone's harassment plan to convince her to give up. "What do you recommend?"

He smiled. "I recommend we fight. Paco mentioned you patrol your place, but if you can afford it, I recommend you increase those patrols. I will win, but it will take time."

She sighed. She was tired of worrying all the time. "I wonder if I will live to see my children grow up to take over the land that rightfully belongs to them?"

He smiled. He had children of his own. They were not lawyers like him, but he understood how a parent would want to leave a legacy to their children.

"That's not the only reason you came though, is it?" she asked, astutely.

He shook his head as he took another sip of the fine, and he suspected, expensive whiskey. "No, we heard from Australia. Their offer has been increased, but they asked for time payments. The preliminary assessment indicates their previous offer wasn't nearly enough. It was much less than the one we have just received. Based on property values, which are very low there, the land isn't worth much, but the improvements, the buildings, the cattle, and the sheep are worth much, much more than they offered."

"So, are they trying to take advantage?" she asked.

He shook his head. "No, I don't think so, not really. If you look at the value and amount of land they have, it's adequate, but it's not an excessive offer. We are looking at the value of everything as a whole and that changes the structure of not only their offer but the station as an asset."

She thought about what Patrick had just told her. Her cousins' offer had been too low, but maybe they didn't realize she would know to assess the value on the stock and improvements. Perhaps, they thought she would only think in terms of land. "Do you know anything about Australia?" she asked him.

He shook his head. "I have the assessor's preliminary information of course, and I have a copy here for you to read." He took a sheaf of papers from an inner pocket and handed it to her as he took a final sip of his whiskey to finish it.

She unfolded it and began to read. There was a knock on the door. Looking up, Carmen called, "Come in?"

A short, squat, Mexican women stuck her head in. "Dinner is on the table," she informed Carmen in Spanish with a big smile, glancing at their visitor.

"Thank you. We will be right there. Have the guest room made up for Senor Larson. He will be staying the night."

The woman nodded as she shut the door.

"Well, let's look at this later when we can discuss it some more," Carmen said in English as she stood up. "Let's go into dinner, shall we?"

CHAPTER FOUR

Carmen looked out at the night from the deep porch that surrounded the hacienda. Her grandfather had built this house, so the cool California nights could be enjoyed. Anyone could sleep out here on the many benches that were scattered around the porches, and they sometimes did. The overhang of the roof concealed her, and anyone watching the house would not be able to see her in the shadows. She frequently walked out on the porches, looking out into the night, just listening and breathing. She regularly wore dark clothes, so she wouldn't stand out like she would in something like a white dress. Tonight, she had a lot on her mind. Should she sell her share of the station to her cousins? That would mean she could collect a percentage of their profits indefinitely. She also worried about the coming fight for the ranch that had been in her family for hundreds of years. She mused over that idea for a very long time.

She heard what she thought was a whisper of a footstep, and her handgun was instantly in her hand as she looked from the corners of her eyes out into the night. One could not look directly at things in the dark. Her cousins knew better than to slip up on the hacienda or even the barns without a whispered shout out. She waited, not moving, knowing movement might give her away and concealment gave her an advantage. She waited a long time, and still, no one came onto the porch. Whatever or whoever it was must have gone away. In the morning, she found a set of boot tracks. Very narrow feet had approached the house and stood there as someone watched the house. They had eventually turned and returned to a cut in the nearby bank where a horse had been waiting and rode away. Carmen was not happy about the fact that someone was this close to her home and her children. She didn't know what they had wanted but considering the news her lawyer had brought her, she could only assume they were up to no good.

She took a buggy out the next day to show Mr. Larson around the immediate area. Although considered a small ranch by California standards, they were gone several hours and still, she had only showed him a small portion of her property. Patrick realized how much this was worth fighting for as he gazed in wonder at the now harvested fruit and the fields of grain where the workers had gone to work next. He admired the beautiful herd of horses that Carmen took such pride in as she explained her program of breeding. It embarrassed him to be talking breeding with a woman, but she was so knowledgeable and natural about it, he found himself impressed and feeling comfortable.

He watched as she used dogs to bring in a herd of cattle along with her magnificent stallion. The love and adoration of the animals was apparent as they were eager to please her. Her children were delightful, ranging in age from ten to three. They were eager to please Carmen as well, and their nurses followed closely behind to keep them in line.

"Carmen, I must say, you have quite a life here. It's worth fighting for!" he said admiringly as they shared a small bottle of locally grown wine.

She nodded. "My family has been on this land for generations. They have no right to take this land from me or my children."

He agreed. It was a life that few people could understand. They were practically self-sufficient out here. "Have you ever considered marrying again?" He knew that with the right marriage, especially to a white man, she would be protected.

She sighed. "I was married to a very weak man. The only good things he gave me were our children." There was a touch of pride in her voice as she mentioned the youngsters, justifiably so he thought. "Being alone since his death, I have had to grow up. I can rely on myself alone."

"But you have your family, your cousins," he objected, gesturing towards the workers they could see in the ranch yard. She was not alone.

She smiled. "They do not own the land. It is mine. They will die defending it for me, but they don't really have that sense of ownership. They too have lived on it for hundreds of years. They are descendants of the original Dons who came here to settle. Some stayed, some married the Indians they found here, and some went back to Mexico or even to Spain. They have pride in the land, but not the responsibility."

She shrugged her delicate shoulders. "Most would not understand. I made the mistake of marrying a good-looking man once, and I won't make the mistake of sharing my responsibility with another. But I grow tired of the fight, Patrick." They had agreed to call each other by their first names. Carmen was technically a middle name but easier on Americans ears. "I know you will be doing the legal fighting for me, but I grow weary of it all."

"What else can you do though, Carmen? You can't give all this up!" His hand took in all the land around them, realizing the immense responsibility that fell on her delicate shoulders.

"I'm thinking a few things over. I'll decide very soon," she told him.

It left him wondering what was going through that fine mind of hers. He had agreed to fight for her, and he would win, but would it be worth the cost?

"She wants what?" Patrick Larson said in consternation a month later.

"She wants us to acquire an ocean-going vessel that will transport horses, people, and household goods. She has decided to go to Australia to claim her inheritance. Apparently, she has sold her family ranch in the valley to a relative, who we have obtained as a client. He has written us too, asking about the impending legal fight for the ranch. She writes to us asking that we obtain passage for her, her children, a few cousins, and her herd of horses," Simon said as though she had lost her mind.

Patrick looked at Simon as though he was the one who had lost his mind and not their client, Carmen.

"Don't shoot the messenger," Simon dared to say.

Patrick smiled sardonically. That was exactly how he was feeling. Carmen hadn't given up the fight. It would continue with the relative, who had bought her ranch. She was going to start anew in Australia. What a brave soul!

CHAPTER FIVE

Packing had been sad. Many memories had gone into boxes and trunks along with their clothing and household goods. Carmen had allowed a fandango to celebrate her cousin's purchase of the ranch. He hadn't expected she would say yes when he had asked her about purchasing the land. He had also expected that upon her acceptance and their signing of the agreement, her impressive herd of horses, especially the stud named Dancer, would be included in the exorbitant purchase price. He was wrong. Having made the long journey from Mexico City to meet this distant cousin, he had had been surprised when she agreed to sell the ranch to him, but he was angry that he hadn't gotten all the stock with the deal. He tried to argue with the American woman after the gold had arrived and had been deposited in the American bank, but he lost, and he wasn't very happy about it.

Still, he had a foothold in the California land, and it wouldn't be his last purchase, if he had his way.

Carmen hadn't intended selling to this cousin, but his sudden appearance and eventual offhand offer for the ranch had seemed like a godsend. She didn't refuse him, and she said if they could agree upon a price, she would indeed sell to him. She knew he had assumed her fantastic herd of horses went with the deal, but nothing was written into their agreement, and once the monies arrived and were deposited into her name, there was nothing cousin Alejandro could do. She had been honest about what had been going on in the valley, telling about the thefts, and they were both confident he could handle it. He thought a man was better suited for this fight, and she just knew she needed to keep her children safe and away from this escalating war. There had been other offers but none as generous and in gold. There would be some bitterness in the valley from those who didn't want another Hispanic coming in, but she and her children would be gone.

"Anyone and their families are welcome to join me. If they don't like Australia, I will allow them to return to America. I only ask that they give it five years, and after that, if they are unhappy, I will pay for their passage back," she told her employees, so many of them distantly related to her. The smiling faces all were loyal to her, and they looked amongst themselves as they immediately began to discuss this opportunity.

This too made Alejandro unhappy, several of her vaqueros, ones he had intended on using for what he considered his ranch now, decided to go with Carmen. If the monies hadn't been transferred out of his account already, he would have somehow taken them back. Instead, he was left trying to fake smile his happiness at this party, this fandango that she insisted on throwing. The Mexican and American music blended badly to his ears. He must keep his anger from spilling over. She could have this win, but if there was some way for him to get the monies back, even the horses that were now well-guarded, he would.

Carmen knew that someone as hard as Alejandro might try to make people bend to his wants and desires for the ranch. She had talked to several of her cousins and employees about him, which was why so many were going with her to try a new life in Australia. One changed his mind at the last minute as his wife would not go because she was afraid of the ocean voyage, and another was staying because he felt his duty was with the land that he had grown up on. Carmen understood and didn't pressure any of them.

The children's nurses all decided to go with her, two of them already eyeing the handsome, tough-looking vaqueros, who would be accompanying their Signora. Some had families, and Carmen arranged wagons for them and their possessions. Their children looked around wide-eyed as they set off on the long trip to San Francisco.

"Carmen, I know this is an adventure to you, but I don't know what you will find there," Patrick Larson warned her as they both watched the many belongings destined for Australia being loaded on the ship he had procured for her use. The horses had gone up the gangway, some with bags over their heads, so they couldn't see where they were going. They were being led by the voices they trusted and were not distracted by the water all around them. Dancer seemed worried about his harem but stood pridefully. He was the last to be loaded and the most dangerous. Dockworkers eyed the nearly wild-looking horse balefully. Carmen personally took the stallion aboard, making sure he was settled in a stall all by himself as she gave him a couple treats. He looked about, his black eyes taking in the familiarity of the stall, but he was not liking that the ground beneath his feet seemed to be swaying. She returned to the pier to watch as the last of her and her companions' household goods were loaded on the ship.

"I'm not worried, Patrick. This is a good decision for me." She told him of her cousin Alejandro, who had fortuitously shown up and how she had outmaneuvered the arrogant Don from Mexico City on her valuable herd of horses. They shared a laugh. "I don't know how receptive he will be to your help in fighting to retain the ranch, but he has your name, and you have his," she discussed with Patrick further.

"He has written to me," he acknowledged. "If ever you decide to return, I hope you know that my services are always available to you and your family," Patrick told her, wondering if something might happen on the long voyage to Australia. So little was known about the interior where she would be settling. Still, her father's brother had settled there and made a station, and he must have left it to her for a reason.

"I thank you, Patrick. Maybe you should come and see it?" she teased with a smile as she watched her people walking up the gangplank, the last of their bundles and supplies in their hands. Several were also holding hands tightly with their children, who looked about wide-eyed at the busy port. Her own children were doing their best to get away from their nurses.

"Ah, that is an adventure I won't ever take," he laughed. He knew he was too old for such a journey. "You will have to write and tell me what it is like."

They finished up the last of their business. He had arranged for some but not all her fortune to be transferred to the Bank of England, so she would have funds available upon her arrival. Knowing that trips such as this could be arduous, they had also made out her will, leaving everything to her children, if they survived. The rest of her estate would go to her people, if there was no direct descendant remaining. She had copies of her will, her letters of introduction, her uncle's will, and a few other documents she would need upon her arrival.

"Well, thank you for your expertise," she said by way of dismissal, not wishing to prolong the goodbye. She signaled to the nurses to get the children on board the ship. She could see the men loading the last of the supplies from the dock.

"Godspeed, Senora Mary Carmen Valenzuela Pearson," he returned, doffing his top hat to her as he relished the Spanish flavor of her complete name.

Carmen laughed, knowing she probably wouldn't hear that again except from her vaqueros or a priest. She began to walk up the plank onto the large ship.

Patrick Larson watched her and the sailors who made the last-minute preparations. Some were pulling in their ropes as they planned to catch the tide, and others were setting small sails to move them out into the bay. The larger sails would be unfurled before they left the large bay that constituted San Francisco, one of the best ports in the world. He had read that Sydney's immense bay rivaled it, but not enough was written about this new country that was still in its infancy.

He turned as the ship began to creep away from the dock. The ropes had been thrown aboard, and the men were climbing either the ropes or the rope ladders. Finally, the plank was pulled onto the ship and they got underway. He waved, and the children waved madly in return. Senora Pearson smiled as she held her three-year-old daughter Rachel in her arms, so she could wave too.

CHAPTER SIX

Carmen, her children, and their nurses were together in a large cabin with bunk beds. The other settlers that had agreed to go with her and the vaqueros, those with wives and families, were billeted in several other cabins like this, some sleeping on the floor. None of them had ever been on a ship before, and there was a period of adjustment as they all got settled.

Most of the supplies, the horses, and the household goods were Carmen's and her people's, but there were trade goods too, and the captain and his men took care of it all. They had experience in transporting livestock, and the horses were well-tended, not only by the sailors but also by Carmen and her people. They were sympathetic to those who immediately experienced seasickness, but there wasn't a lot that could be done for these people other than supplying them with

buckets and fresh water. Water would be limited to the many barrels they had on board for the stock and people. Any rain that could be gathered would go into empty barrels as they accumulated. This many people and animals would consume a lot of water, and the captain had planned accordingly when he took on this commission. He didn't know who Senora Pearson was, but she must be important to be able to pay for most of his ship's cargo area and for all the people and their supplies. Mr. Larson, who had contacted and then contracted with him on her behalf, had negotiated a good deal all around. Captain Jamieson was certain he could get the cargo and all these people and their animals safely across the vast ocean.

"Captain," Carmen nodded as she greeted the man, looking out at the horizon as San Francisco had retreated behind them many hours ago. There was nothing but water around them or an occasional boat or ship heading back in the direction they had come.

"Senora Pearson," he greeted her, looking out at the deck and his men scurrying about doing their duties. His eyes were perpetually squinted from long days at sea and a lifetime of sailing ships. His eyes missed little as he scanned his ship from the high deck, known as a poop deck. His hands were sure and steady on the large wheel. His first mate stepped up and relieved him of the wheel, and he joined the woman at the rail. "Beautiful, isn't it?" he inquired as she gazed out at the endless sea. The sun was shining brightly as they were long gone from the endless fogs that frequently enfolded the large city of San Francisco.

"Fascinating," she murmured, wondering if this move had been a mistake. But she was committed, for better or for worse.

"You aren't suffering from mal de mer?" he teased, smiling and showing teeth slightly stained from tea and tobacco.

She smiled. Despite his use of the French term, she understood what he was asking. The last two words sounded the same in both French and Spanish. "No, I don't seem to be suffering from dolor de mar," she responded, giving the expression the full inflection and richness of the Spanish language. Her Spanish, which she could switch from the Americanized or Hispanic to the Castilian that she had learned at her mother and grandfather's knee, sounded natural coming out of her mouth. "How long is the voyage, Capitán?" she asked teasingly since he wanted to play with words.

He laughed. His skills in various languages were a necessity as he shipped goods around the world. He understood she had enjoyed his teasing. "If we keep our winds," he answered in Americanized English while looking up into the full sails his men were maintaining, "it should be about one hundred fifty days or so. We may stop in Tahiti or somewhere for fresh water, if we don't get enough rain, which would delay us either way."

"It looks so calm and so peaceful," she said as she looked back out to sea, watching the reflections of the sun on the rippling water. The waves were not too rough as the large ship plowed its way through the deep waters, its sails filled with the winds that would could carry her across this immense ocean.

"Aye, it is now, but the sea can be a capricious bitch when she wants. Don't ever count on her," he told her, searching in his pockets for his pipe and tobacco.

"I imagine the storms out here can be terrible," she understated as she watched him fill and light his pipe, cupping his hand against the eternal winds and using his body as a further bulwark to protect the flame, so it could fire the tobacco. Practice had him puffing away on his pipe in no time at all as she watched.

"Aye, they can be," he agreed, talking around the stem of his well-worn pipe. "I've seen waves so large they seemed like mountains of water."

"Will we be seeing any of those?" she asked, suddenly aware that everything and everyone she cared for was on this ship. She was feeling very helpless as she looked out at the seemingly calm ocean.

"Let's pray not, madam," he told her, glancing to see how alarmed he had made her. He'd noted the tone in her voice that told him he had frightened her, but her face revealed nothing. "I won't lie to you. If we get a storm, and we probably will, you will have to tie down your horses, your children, and your people. Our job," he said, nodding towards the men diligently working about the ship, "is to keep this ship afloat and get us to Sydney."

Carmen had understood that. She'd seen the straps on the bunks and explained their purpose to her people. She'd worried that some might want to leave, but everyone had been given a chance to stay in their familiar valley and had still chosen to go with her as she emigrated to Australia. She nodded in agreement to the captain's statement.

Two days later, a storm did hit. Fortunately for them, it was mild and provided them with more water to fill the few casks that had already been emptied in their endless demand for fresh water. Carmen and her people, including the vaqueros, grooms, and settlers, helped where they could. The horses' stalls were cleaned daily of the piles the animals made, and the manure was thrown over the side. A limited supply of straw for bedding necessitated that they only clean up the debris and not replace the entire bedding each time. Used to freedom on the plains of the large, inland valley and not being cooped up in the ship as it rode the waves sometimes caused frayed tempers in the large beasts. Carmen frequently found herself rushing from her children to her babies (her horses) and calming both with her presence and caresses.

When the seas were calm enough, they briefly walked the horses one by one up and down the small passageway in order to exercise them twice a day. It wasn't nearly enough, but it kept the horses from standing too long in their stalls. Dancer was becoming even more fractious, and only Carmen could keep him from biting people in anger over being confined.

"There, there," she soothed him in both English and Spanish, whispering sweet nothings to the great beast. She loved him, and he seemed to understand her.

"Mama, can I help with Dancer?" Philippe asked, and she looked up from her murmurings with her stud to smile at her oldest son, who looked like a young Don standing there, her grandfather, skipping a generation.

"Not now, Philippe. He is just angry," she told him in English as she turned back to the mighty beast, patting him affectionately and calming him. "Aren't you, fellow?" she asked him. He seemed to nod, agreeing with her. She knew he would always agree with her because she never asked him anything he would disagree with. He was her

baby, and she glanced at the many mares she had brought with her as well as geldings, sons of Dancer's that weren't quite up to par with their mighty stud. They had brought coach horses, riding horses, and special mounts belonging to her men as well. She knew she could have purchased more horses in Australia, but since she'd hired this ship to transport her stock, she had indulged a few of her men in their own mounts since there had been room.

"He is angry a lot these days," the boy noted, watching as she caressed the large horse. Dancer was a special friend to the boy, and he was proud that he and his siblings had been singled out as friends by the mighty beast. Others back at the hacienda had been in awe of their ability to touch the great animal. He'd seen Dancer go after anyone that dared to come into his fields, near his harem, or attempt to harm anything he considered his. He knew two men had died trying to steal this stallion.

"He is just tired of being confined," she agreed. Carmen patted the stallion as she slipped him a carrot and backed away to concentrate on her son. "Have you finished your schoolwork?" she asked, putting her arm around the boy and leading him back down the aisle towards the stairs where their own accommodations were located. The stallion crunched happily, watching *his* people walking away.

"Mama, must I study? We–" he began but could feel her arm reflexively squeeze him.

"You will study your entire life. I want a college education for you someday," she told him, not for the first time.

"My father did not have one," he pointed out reasonably.

"No, he did not, and you are not your father. However, your grandfather was an educated man, and he is someone you should emulate."

"What is emulate?"

"See, if you studied, you would know that word."

"Maybe I know it in Spanish and not English?" he asked slyly.

She laughed at him, not falling for his neat little trap. "You must set an example for your brothers and sister, and studying is part of that. Every day, you must learn something, even if it's just a little something. Someday, that knowledge will come in handy."

"I hardly think that learning how to dissect a sentence in both English and Spanish will benefit me as an adult."

"Perhaps, perhaps not. You won't know until it comes up, will you?" she pointed out as she opened the door to the dormitory style room they shared. She smiled in welcome at the various women, who were going about their business inside the room. She could see two of her children, five-year-old Nicolás and three-year-old Rachel, were playing. They were rolling a ball, but not with their own hands. The roll of the ship sent the ball back and forth, causing them great hilarity as they tried to keep it from going off course. She gave Philippe a slight push towards the bunk he shared with his brothers, and he went to pull out a grammar book from his box of books. "Where is Sebastián?" she asked the room at large, wondering where the seven-year-old had gotten to. She noticed one of the nurses was also missing and hoped she was with the young boy.

"He has finished his studies, and Gabriela took him up on deck to breathe the fresh air. Reading makes him green, Senora," one of the women immediately answered, looking up and wondering if Carmen was going to be angry.

Compassion filled Carmen. She knew that her little Sebby had not been faring well on this voyage due to seasickness. It had hit several of their people, but they had no choice. There was no turning back now. She nodded as she went to leave the crowded room.

"Mama, may we come?" asked Nicolás in a small boy's voice, his hand pulling on her skirt.

Carmen looked down at her hopeful son and asked, "Come where?"

"Are you going to find Sebby?" he asked, and behind him Rachel nodded solemnly in agreement.

"I am. Would you and Rachel like to go up top with me?"

He nodded seriously.

"Then put away your ball. You can't take a ball up on deck. Someone might slip on it, or it might roll off the ship," she told him, watching as he ran to put it away, pulling out his small box from under the bunk and dropping it inside. Holding both her son and daughter's hands, she was followed by a couple of the women, one with a son of her own held in her arms. Carmen made her way carefully up the stairs. Unable to lift her skirt because of the children, she kicked each of her legs up before taking another stair. It probably looked odd, but she didn't want to trip and take the children down with her.

The captain had designated part of the deck for his passengers to walk about, keeping them well away from the sails and the sailors working above deck. Some of the sailors were not very kind or gallant to the many women sailing with them. Some were even a bit base, but they had learned to curb their impulses because the captain was willing to whip them for their temerity in speaking in an ungentlemanly-like manner. One of their own had learned the first week that the captain would allow no harassment of the women or children under his care, and it had served as an example to the rest of the men, who avoided the passengers as well as they could. Naturally, their work brought them into near proximity of the women, children, men, and animals under their care on the ship. The captain realized the importance of Senora Pearson, who had paid for most of their ship's cargo space and still allowed him to procure some other cargo for trade and cartage, and he also realized she was not to be harassed in any manner. Her vaqueros would not tolerate it, and there were always at least one or two vaqueros surrounding the woman, who were quite touchy and quick to take insult. Another of his men had earned their ire and nearly gone overboard as they whipped him with their whips and beat him with their hands. They were not large men, but they were certainly quick to take offence and react regarding their senora.

Carmen loved being up on deck when the weather was pleasant, and she shepherded her children before her, watching them carefully and keeping them well away from the sides. She had instructed their nurses to keep them from this barely safe barrier, but the boys seemed drawn to it. The boys wanted to lean over and watch the water going by. They were fascinated by it and kept putting themselves into danger. She wasn't even aware that Paco and Jose walked several paces behind her skirts. She was so used to her cousins' presence, she didn't even realize they were there. When she 'saw' Paco, she asked him how the horses were faring. She was worried and didn't want to lose any of her valuable babies on this long and arduous trip. So far, other than a general restlessness, they were doing well.

"Ma'am," the Captain addressed her, putting his hand to his hat out of respect as he doffed it and returned it his head.

"Captain, it's a pleasure to see you as always. What can I do for you today?" she asked, smiling her greeting.

"I have decided to put in at the Sandwich Islands for water, fresh fruit, and vegetables," he informed her, watching her with her children. She did not look at any of the men on the ship, and he was grateful she wasn't making any trouble for him in that way. One of her nurses was, but he wasn't certain Carmen knew the woman was a harlot. He glanced at the vaquero watching him, his hands near his belt, the dangerous looking whip, and a knife that would do any sailor proud. He'd heard several of his men trying to barter with the Californios in hopes of trading for these beauties but to no avail.

"And what are the Sandwich Islands?" she asked, looking interested after all the weeks at sea.

He explained they were islands that had been discovered by the famed explorer Captain Cook in 1778. Most ships sailing the Pacific found them a convenient stopping point for the very reasons he told her: water, fruit, and vegetables. He did not tell her that his men had been looking forward to sampling the native women, who were so accommodating to men from all over the world. He himself would wait for Sydney, not taking chances on a diseased woman and knowing of a brothel that was known for clean and pox-free women.

"Will we be able to put the horses ashore and allow them to graze and run about?" she asked anxiously, hopefully. She wanted to keep them healthy and happy, and their restlessness was not good.

"No, ma'am. We won't have the time, not if we are to keep to the schedule I agreed upon in my contract with you and your lawyer," he told her. He knew his men would be disappointed, at least some of them would be since they wouldn't be there long enough for all of them to indulge in some time off from their almost constant duties.

"Captain, I would like to take the time. If there is any way to take the horses ashore, I would appreciate the consideration. My horses are very valuable, as you know. I'm sure we would all appreciate a few days on this island," she indicated the few passengers on deck as well as his sailors hurrying about.

He smiled, not having considered staying more than the necessary time to restock their water and food. She might regret it as there were natives who would covet the fine horses, and he knew they were not for sale…she had made that clear when she insisted on bringing them along. He wondered if he would lose any of his men by being in this exotic port too long and made a mental note to tell his officers to tighten discipline of the men. They would get time off and have plenty of time to seek out diversions, but their honor and their ethics might be tested if the ship remained too long. He didn't want any men to desert him as he would then be forced to take on new men he didn't know and trust. It was important to him as the captain that he trust his men. "Yes, ma'am. I am sure we can accommodate you," he agreed, doffing his hat again as he excused himself from her presence. He nodded to the two vaqueros, their faces giving nothing away as they looked at him, their black eyes boring holes in him.

CHAPTER SEVEN

Everyone seemed to be looking forward to the rest stop on the islands. Some of the sailors shared stories of times they had been there before and the beauty of the islands. As they were not allowed to talk to the women, the men shared these stories with the male travelers, who passed them along, although some of what they had been told was edited out.

Carmen would never forget her first view of the island they were approaching. She'd heard shouts of absolute delight from the sailors up top and couldn't wait to get dressed and see for herself. Since the captain had said they would stop there, she had her men ask the sailors for information, and she was excited by what they would see.

They had learned that the Sandwich Islands were originally named by Captain Cook because he was honoring John Montagu. John

Montagu was the fourth Earl of Sandwich and had been one of Captain Cook's sponsors as the first Lord of the Admiralty. Now, they were regularly calling them the Hawaiian Islands. It was all so fascinating with people from all over the world, the natives, the exotic foods, and the islands themselves. Apparently, they were an archipelago of eight major islands, several atolls, and numerous islets and seamounts.

"They go for over 1500 miles," the captain contributed to the curiosity of the Californians. He went on to explain that they were the exposed peaks of a great undersea mountain range. "They were originally formed by volcanos, and there is still an active volcano."

"And would you say this is the halfway point of our trip?" she asked as she ignored her meal while they were discussing this fascinating stop in their trip.

"Oh, no, ma'am," he answered, sorry to disillusion her. "We've only come about thirty-eight hundred nautical miles."

"And how much farther is Sydney?" she asked, feeling that she had no concept of the miles traveled when traveling by sea.

"Sydney is another eight thousand miles or so."

Carmen felt crushing disappointment. Knowing that her people were already tired of the trip, she decided she wouldn't inform them. Paco and Julio, who were eating with them at the captain's table along with her children and their nurses, looked disappointed as well. She wouldn't let it keep her down though. It was important that her people keep their spirits up. "You said there are several islands. Do they have names?"

"Yes, Hawaii is the largest of the islands. This is where we will stop for our supplies, and I'll arrange to unload your horses for a few days. We will have to make arrangements for them to be fed and exercised," he told her. He was certain such things could be arranged, having discussed it several times with her. "There is a town building up there that I'm certain will fascinate you and your company." His eyes took in the two vaqueros watching him and making sure he made no inappropriate comments to the lady. He was certain these men, menacing in their countenance, would have no problem running him through, if he dared. He knew how to behave like a gentleman and wouldn't have ventured to make a pass at this fascinating woman. The ranch she and her family had owned in the great inland valley in California sounded just as fascinating to him as Australia and Hawaii now sounded to her.

"Then there are the other, smaller islands of Maui, O'ahu, Kaua'i, Molok'i, Lãna'I, Ni'ihau, and Kaho'olawe," he told her, giving the names the correct inflections and nuance having learned them on previous trips to this region of the world.

"What are the people like, the natives?" she asked, endlessly finding topics of discussion as they shared meals and her interest in their first stop grew.

Arranging for forage for the horses proved quite easy as there were many farms on the island. The horses, many of the black mix of breeds, caused a sensation. Carmen could see the admiration on people's faces as she rode Dancer along, helping to bring her babies to the farm they had rented for the few days they would be there. Several of her vaqueros would remain with them, switching out with those guarding the Senora in order to see more of the island.

The children came off the ship along with her people, who took up residence at the farmhouse for the few days they were staying. They loved being able to run freely in the fields that the farm encompassed.

The women shopped in the town where they found exotic foods and tried a new fruit called pineapple. It was very sweet but had a hard rind that one of the natives showed them how to slice with a machete.

The captain allowed his men off the ship in shifts, so they would all have the benefit of some off time from the endless work aboard a ship. He left plenty on board to guard their valuable cargo as well as to ensure they had men when it was time to leave.

"Ahoy there, Jamieson," a fellow captain greeted him as he went into one of the many bars set up in the town. "Let's have a pint," he offered generously, signaling to the serving wench and patting her on the backside when she brought them both a frothy tankard. "What have you on this trip? Did I see horses being off-loaded?"

"Aye, I have passengers and stock heading for Australia," he answered, taking a hearty drink of the beer they were served. He wanted to grimace. He'd had better but knew not to be too choosy.

"Are they for King Kamehameha?" the man inquired, obviously having already drunk several tankards of the beer.

"Nay, they are owned by one of the settlers. We decided a couple days ashore would be beneficial to them and their people." He didn't like sharing the information, but it was impossible to hide that many fine horses, and they had made quite an impression coming ashore. He knew the vaqueros guarding the animals might have to defend themselves from those who thought to help themselves to the animals and the women. This place could be a cesspool.

"You know, if the King's people see them, they may want them," the man said warningly, finishing his beer and signaling for another.

The captain hadn't really worried about the king and his people, having only thought of other sailors from around the world that inhabited the dregs of society and whose only goal was to futter as many of the native women as they could find. He nodded to acknowledge the other captain and slowly finished his own tankard. Now, he was worried about Senora Pearson and her damned horses. He left the bar as soon as he could without insulting the other captain. He sought out a couple of his officers and sent them to warn the Senora and her men to be extra vigilant.

The restocking of water, food, and fodder for the horses took no time at all but waiting for the horses to eat their fill and for everyone to enjoy their time ashore seemed to make the days in port drag. Captain Jamieson cut his own free time short in order that a few more of his men could enjoy themselves. Several returned early, having overindulged, and they were puking up the contents of their stomachs as they sought their bunks or hammocks. After a week in port, the longest he could remember being there, he was delighted to see the Californians and their stock coming down the large pier and being reloaded on the ship. Some of the horses balked. They had liked their time ashore and were not willing to go back into the familiar cargo hold. He had his sailors help the vaqueros, surprised that Senora Pearson herself sweet-talked not only her stallion but several other of the fractious horses into coming aboard. Still, some did have to have their heads hooded to hide the sight of water on both sides of the ramp.

The passengers were finally settled, and they cast off, well stocked for the next part of their trip. Everyone seemed refreshed from their stopover.

"Captain, I am curious," Senora Pearson addressed him, looking at the rather crude maps that showed the seas and land backwards. There were few details other than major ports and towns on the land side, but

many notes, including depths, longitude, and latitude visible on the large papers. She pointed to New Zealand. "Why we don't head for this before Australia?"

"With the curve of the Earth, it isn't like a straight line. There are winds to consider as well as other obstacles, such as currents that can help or hinder our passage," he explained, delighted in the intelligence of this woman. She came across as simple but was far from it, and her looks had been commented on by his men many times. She was intelligent, and it was obvious her children had inherited this intelligence from her as they were just as inquisitive when they had the captain's ear.

The voyage continued. It was long, and many storms impeded their way. His passengers were by turn ill from being thrown about by the massive waves or on deck taking in the air in order to get some time out of the cabins assigned to them. The ship was becoming rather gamy to them all since there were animals and their resulting odors, despite the constant cleaning of their stalls. They'd taken on fresh fodder for the many beasts in Hawaii, and this had helped. Apparently, the animals had all benefited from going ashore as had the people.

They stopped in Tahiti, the halfway point between Hawaii and Australia, but the captain would not allow the horses ashore on this island. These natives weren't like the natives on the island of Hawaii. They were a bit primitive, and he didn't trust some of the men who lived there. The island was claimed by the French, traditional enemies of the English, so the captain had to walk a fine line. He and his ship were American, but the natives had been known to impose taxes and even confiscate some things. He kept a low profile and kept his men in check, only allowing one night off for each of the shifts. They took on more water and supplies and even managed to get more fresh fodder for the horses before they quickly continued their journey.

CHAPTER EIGHT

They were all relieved to finally see the headlands that formed the over one-mile-wide entrance to Sydney. Captain Jamieson pointed out North Head and Quarantine Head to his passengers. He explained that there was also South Head and Dunbar Head, pointing south where they would have been visible had they come from that direction. They had traveled to Australia through the Tasman Sea, keeping well out to avoid what was now called The Great Barrier Reef as well as smaller reefs that protected this land mass. Once in the harbor they saw Middle, Georges, and Chowder Head. He pointed out the various islands as the sailors took in their great sails to slow their ship.

"I'll have to weigh anchor and make arrangements for docking. That can take some time in this busy port," he informed Senora Pearson. "A lot of ships use porters," he indicated the smaller boats, barges, and modest platforms where goods were ferried to and from the ships. "I wouldn't advise that for the horses and your people…unless, you are anxious?" he began, seeing the alarmed look in the woman's face.

Carmen sighed. "It has been a long five months," she admitted, cheering up as their destination was in sight. They'd passed the original fort Port Jackson, and the captain had pointed it out.

"It would be best that we got your horses to the stockyards to keep them until you can make arrangements to go to your station," he told her, and she nodded.

It took less time to find a dock where they could unload stock than the captain had anticipated. They offloaded the horses and then the many household goods and cargo the Californios had brought with them. The captain helped to arrange rental of a warehouse to house the people and their goods until they made further arrangements. He couldn't help with that after he took his leave of them. He was sad to see them go; it had been an interesting trip with the many personalities. He wished the Senora well on her travels to her station. Turning away, he left to arrange to unload the rest of his ship and find cargo he could take back to the states on their return journey.

"We will have to find out where Twin Station is and see if anyone is heading in that direction," Carmen decided, discussing it with Paco. Already, their horses had engendered much interest in the stockyards. People were trying to buy them. One had even attempted to walk off with a couple, and after this attempt to steal them, the Senora had several of the vaqueros guarding her babies. They took her children, their nurses, and their baggage and sought a respectable hotel. Checking in, Carmen also inquired about banks in the area and presented her letters of introduction to the Bank of England, who had received notice of the funds transferred to Mrs. Pearson's accounts. That handled, she returned to the hotel for dinner. Their group took up an entire table, only a few absent as some of her men stayed to guard their people and her horses in the warehouse. She'd arranged for fresh food to be brought to them.

They discussed Sydney and what they had seen so far, talking rapidly in Spanish as their food was delivered. Carmen had been fascinated by the different foliage and wondered if her horses would adapt well to the fodder they had managed to obtain at the stockyards. The hay and grain looked the same, but Australia felt so different. They were all on edge, and she was certain her horses felt it too.

Seeing the dark looks that were aroused by their speaking Spanish, Carmen effortlessly switched to English, her voice distinct and containing a hint of the Latina inflections as she spoke to her men. One had asked what they would do if they couldn't find a guide out to Twin Station. "We'll have to find my cousins' lawyer and see about taking a wagon and supplies out to the station," she said to him.

"Do you think we should bring stock to the station?" one of the men asked her.

"Perhaps. I don't know how many sheep they have out there, but I want to be sure to contribute."

"Your horses should be enough of a contribution," one of the older men was saying, his dark moustache tinged with a bit of gray.

"I can't believe the brazen attempts to take my horses away," she said, lowering her voice so only her men would hear her. "It was a good idea to leave some of the men to guard my babies."

A couple of the men had looked around, always on guard where the Senora was concerned. They had seen one man listening unashamedly and frowned at him, trying to warn him off. The conversation at the table switched effortlessly from English back to Spanish.

A large man approached their table. "Ma'am," he said, taking off the stockman's hat he had just put on after getting up from his own table. "I couldn't help but overhear your accent. You are from California?"

Carmen looked up and saw the tall man, who whipped off his hat politely. He too had an American accent, and she smiled politely. "Yes, we are," she said in an inquiring tone.

"I am Mel Lawrence," he told her politely. "I'm originally from the east coast, but I have been through your beautiful state. I couldn't help but overhear you are going out to a station?" he asked, including the glowering vaqueros as he looked around. He knew that a strange man didn't usually approach a Hispanic woman, and this woman was particularly well-guarded.

"I am Carmen Pearson," the woman said, her slight accent sounding beautiful to Mel and further enhancing her natural good looks. She put out a hand that Mel captured, intending to shake and then, on impulse, lifted to kiss the back as he had seen men do. He grinned unrepentedly as she saw the men bristle.

Carmen was amused. It was so gallant and so old-fashioned. She saw her men didn't like the strange man but that was on principle as they were here to protect her. Since many of them were distant cousins of her mother's, they felt it their duty. "What brings you to Australia, Mr. Lawrence?" she asked, her eyes twinkling.

"I was shanghaied outside of San Francisco," he admitted, speaking low in case they were overheard. "It's a long story, but I've decided to stay. I too am heading inland. When I heard an accent from back home, I couldn't help but make your acquaintance."

"That's very kind of you, Mr. Lawrence. I would love to hear your story?" she answered, intrigued by the large man. There was something about him, but she couldn't quite put her finger on it. Perhaps it was just that he was a stranger. She waved to indicate a vacant chair.

"I would love to speak with you, but I must seek my bed. It has been a long day for me, and I have business to attend to in the morning. Will you be staying in Sydney long?"

"Only a few days, just long enough to rest. I brought a herd of horses, and they must get settled after that long boat ride before we set off to our station. Perhaps we will see each other again, and you can tell me more of your story then?"

"I would like that, Miss Pearson."

"Oh, it's Mrs. Pearson," she corrected automatically.

Mel had already noticed that there was no ring on her finger but accepted her word. He nodded, acknowledging the new term of address. "Good night, Mrs. Pearson." He smiled towards the still glowering men, nodding towards them as well as he included them in his farewell, then he bowed slightly towards the woman and excused himself.

"That was forward," Paco hissed before he could help himself, his moustache bristling angrily.

Carmen cocked an eyebrow towards her segundo, and he squirmed almost immediately. Since they had left the Americas, he had felt very protective towards his employer. It was a self-inflicted duty, but he felt fatherly towards her. They were distantly related, as were almost all her men, and it meant they were all loyal to her. "Paco do not presume to direct my behavior. He was polite, he was interesting, and perhaps he can give us information from his own observations in this foreign land."

He blushed as he nodded, accepting her criticism as his due. They finished their meal, feeling the food could have used some more spices.

CHAPTER NINE

Carmen found the lawyer after her men made inquiries for her. He wasn't pleased to see the American woman. He knew his clients had wanted to buy her out, and her presence meant he had failed. He wasn't sure how to help direct her to the ranch, which they called a station out here. He said he would keep his ear out for someone heading that way, but they both knew he was only giving her lip service. She left the solicitor's office very unhappy with the experience.

"Now what, Senora?" Paco asked when she relayed what the solicitor had told her.

"I think we should start inquiries by sending the men to the inns and pubs," she smiled, knowing she was using the British terms instead of their own American words for hotels and taverns. It was deliberate as they were now here in this new land, for better or worse. "Have them inquire as to anyone who might know of Twin Station and how to get there."

A few days later, Carmen was at the stockyard checking on her babies, who were obviously happy to be off the ship and becoming a bit restless. Already, Dancer had kicked out some fencing in anger over someone trying to touch *his* harem. She was amused and gladly paid for the damages her baby had caused. She knew they couldn't stay in Sydney indefinitely, and while she had explored the city a bit on Dancer and accompanied by several of her men, they needed to get going. Judging by the length of time it took a letter to get from the station to Sydney and then to San Francisco and the ranch, she suspected they still had quite a journey ahead of them. She was pleased to see the other American, Mel Lawrence, at the stockyards. She watched as the man, dressed in stockmen's clothes that were much different from the fine suit he had been wearing back at the hotel the other night, appeared to negotiate for some dogs. She wondered what he intended to do and wanted desperately to talk to a fellow American. She smiled as she saw the American walk away with four dogs. She lost sight of him but watched for him on the days she visited the stockyards to check up on her horses and walked to the warehouse to check on her people. She was pleased when a few days later she spotted the American at the stockyards once again.

"Buying up Australia?" Carmen teased when she walked up to the fence where the American was looking over some animals. They didn't look very good to the experienced rancher, and she wondered what Mel's interest was in them.

"Mrs. Pearson, it's always a delight to see you," Mel returned as he turned from the animals he was perusing. The sheep looked terrible with their long wooly coats shorn, some with splotches of wool still on them and others with nicks and cuts from the shears. He lifted his hat respectfully but didn't remove it in the hot Australian sun.

"Do you know where you are going in the Outback?" Carmen inquired, glancing at the stock and shaking her head slightly.

"I'm not sure yet. I thought I'd go to the end of the tracks and on into the never-never," he admitted, the thought not so far from his actual plans. He glanced at the sheep in the corral and frowned slightly. They wouldn't be worth taking into the Outback; he was certain they wouldn't survive.

"We are going out to the station I own with my distant cousins. Why don't we travel together?"

"Your men wouldn't like that," he pointed out, glancing towards two of them that were far enough away to give the woman privacy, but close enough to guard her in the event a man approached her. They did not look happy about Carmen approaching the American.

"No, they wouldn't; however, that doesn't dictate my actions, and we do have to get going. I've spent enough time here in Sydney. I was hoping to buy some sheep too," she indicated the poor animals in one of the corrals near where they were standing.

"Slim pickings," Mel mentioned, and just then, a commotion near the front of the stockyards drew both their attention. His dogs were sitting around his feet, panting, and they perked up at the mass of sheep that men were even now putting in several corrals.

"What's going on?" Carmen murmured as they both started walking towards the uproar.

"I have no idea," Mel stated as he signaled to the four dogs, who followed at his feet instantly. He hadn't made them work since he bought them, but they did guard his wagon for him when he fed them and left them to return to the hotel nightly. He hadn't had a moment to seek out the woman from California but still wished to talk to her.

The dust the sheep kicked up was intense and both Mel and Carmen used handkerchiefs to cover their mouths and noses. Carmen's handkerchief was a delicate Queen Anne piece of lace and Mel's was a red bandana that reminded him of America, which he had found in a store.

"What's going on?" Mel asked one of the men as he closed a paddock that was packed with the sheep they had just herded in.

"Bank confiscation," he said with a grin, glancing at Carmen more than once and hoping to catch her eye.

"What does that mean?" Mel asked for them both, suddenly feeling protective of Carmen. Glancing around, he was not surprised to see Paco and one of the other men a few paces off.

"Some bloke ordered these from England. He ran outta money before they arrived, and the bank confiscated 'em."

Mel looked at the sheep. They were Merinos, the very breed that a man by the name of Foster had told him were one of the best for wool production. The sheep in the other paddocks paled by comparison. These also had full coats and hadn't been sheared of the long coats on their bodies. "How many are there?" he asked, speculating as he eyed them.

"Over five thousand," he bragged, still trying to catch Carmen's eye but failing. Still, he answered Mel as though he were speaking on behalf of the Hispanic beauty.

"Who do I talk to about buying 'em?" he asked. Carmen perked up at this question, looking intently to hear the answer.

"Yank, yer gonna have to wait for the auction just like everyone else," he said as he turned to hurry and help with the other sheep being loaded in another of the paddocks. They were filling the small space end to end with the poor animals.

"I'll go halves," Carmen murmured as she saw Mel's determined look.

Mel turned to look down on the petite woman in surprise. He had forgotten she was there as he thought about what obtaining the sheep would mean.

Just then, more sheep and more men arrived. Neither Mel nor Carmen had ever seen the stockyards this full, but it explained the many pens that had lain empty. The stockyard could easily accommodate thousands of animals. Mel looked down at his dogs. They were shaking with excitement at the idea of helping, and he could tell they were barely constrained and only obeying him because he had fed them, and they were now loyal to him.

"Let's see what else we can find out," he advised, and Carmen nodded. Mel wanted all five thousand sheep for himself but didn't know if he could handle that many alone. He wasn't ready to hire other shepherds, or stockmen as the Australians called them, to work for him just yet. He didn't even know where he was going.

It was Paco who learned there were eight thousand sheep and which bank owned them. Mel and Carmen headed for that bank to ask about purchasing them outright and not waiting for the auction. Mel had a good idea how much they were worth unshorn and discussed it with the woman as they rode towards the bank. Two of her men followed them, guarding the senora and looking menacingly towards any who would look sideways at the woman. The four dogs followed Mel's horses' hooves, keeping an eye out, so they didn't get trampled, but Mel figured they could use the exercise, and he wanted to keep them away from the temptation of the sheep.

"They are to go up for auction," the bank manager stated loftily when they approached him.

"Mr. Allen, I'm sure I could make this easier for you," Mel stated. "Your bank stands to lose money on the deal since the owner forfeited them."

"How did you–?" he began, but Mel interrupted, lifting a hand to silence the man, something a woman wouldn't have dared or been allowed to get away with. The banker glanced from the large man to the petite woman next to Mel.

"I'm sure you understand how these rumors get started. The animals have just come from a long voyage and are in poor shape. You are going to have to have them sheared, if they survive, and then of course, their value is halved after shearing." Mel and Carmen both saw him start at the phrase *'if they survive.'* "We are willing to pay you for them outright," he dangled the offer.

"I don't even know you…" he began, suspicious of the Yank's accent as well as the dusky beauty who accompanied him and remained silent.

"You can check with the Bank of England. My account will be used for this transaction, and they will assure you I have the funds," he said firmly, using the snobby tone he had acquired defensively back in his days in New York.

"And you are…?"

"Mel Lawrence," he returned, not even thinking of using his full name with Carmen Pearson listening.

The banker had heard the name. Bankers congregated often, and a Yank transferring funds to the Bank of England branch here in Sydney had been titillating gossip. The name didn't sound quite right, but it had been awhile since it was discussed, and he could be remembering it wrong. "Would you be willing to pay what they are worth in England?"

"Come now, man. They have just gotten off a ship from England. They barely survived the crossing and look terrible." Actually, they had looked good, considering the trip. It was obvious they had been well taken care of. "If I take them–" he began but Carmen interrupted.

"We," she breathed, clutching at Mel's elbow slightly to remind him that she was there.

Mel looked down and saw the twinkle in the woman's eye. She knew he was bargaining with the banker and was not fooled at all. The banker, however, didn't know stock. By the time they agreed to buy the entire flock as is, they had wheedled the price down considerably, but it was a cash deal, and the banker felt pleased for having gotten anything for the poor, diseased, and apparently dying sheep. He accepted a bank draft from both Americans, each paying for half the deal and signed the animals over to them.

"Now, what?" Carmen asked with a grin as they left the bank, each holding firmly to the bills of sale with both their names on them.

"I guess we get our sheep sheared and finish stocking up for the trip out to your station. I'll see what I can find nearby when we split up the flock."

"Maybe you will be one of my neighbors," Carmen said generously, having no idea what she would find when she got out to Twin Station where her cousins were running the sheep station. They were her reluctant partners, and she wondered how they would feel about her purchase. The lawyer here in Sydney had tried to get her to sell out several times since she had arrived. She'd perversely stayed in the large city to get the lay of the land, but it was time she headed out. Her men would be pleased as they were restless.

"Maybe," Mel agreed, delighted with their purchase. It was a great bargain, and they congratulated each other as they headed back to the stockyards.

They disappointed quite a few people, who had looked forward to buying some of the sheep and were hoping to get a bargain themselves. When they found out the auction was completely off because two Yanks had bought the entire flock, it created some ill will. Mel watched as they sheep were sheared, wanting to learn how to do it himself. He was disappointed that some of the ill will towards his and Carmen's purchase from under the noses of more experienced grazers continued as the shearers swore at, nicked, and treated their sheep badly. Carmen watched as well, learning an aspect of animal husbandry she knew would be valuable on the sheep station where she was heading.

"Easy there. Either cut him evenly or get another job," Mel warned one of the shearers menacingly when he saw the slipshod job he was doing.

"Yeah? Whatcha going to do about it?" the shearer challenged, rising from where he had been bending over the sheep he was shearing.

Mel didn't hesitate. He knew that waiting and posturing was pointless. He hit the man, one hard right to his unprotected jaw, and he went down. He seemed to fly as he also tripped over the downed sheep he had been shearing, and he was out cold. Mel looked around for other troublemakers, but the other shearers got busy over their own animals and began clipping a little more carefully as they took off the sheep's long, wool coats.

"I don't think we'll have any more problems with them," Carmen commented after she observed her partner taking down that man. Mel hadn't followed through with the man, and one of his mates had picked the stunned man up from the floor when he began to come around. He had gone back to work, doing a better and more careful job from then on.

The men got paid according to how many sheep they clipped, no matter how long the coats or how quickly they did it. Eight thousand sheep were quickly defrocked, and the wool was taken away to be shipped to England and the mills there.

Mel and Carmen both filled wagons with supplies, peas, rice, salt pork, flour, and other necessities that were frequently shipped inland to the various stations. Mel met the rest of the dozen men Carmen had traveling with her as they readied for the long trip. Some had families of their own, and he found himself liking them. Carmen's children were a hoot, but their nursemaids seemingly disapproved of the Yank they had heard so much about from the men. A guide, who had been to Twin Station before and was returning with their annual supplies, agreed to travel with the Americans and show them the way. Several wagons, Mel's included, which Carmen bought from him, left the stockyards and met up with the drayage company's wagons. Mel had

purchased two more dogs and Carmen found five, so there were eleven dogs surrounding the flock as they set out. Another dog was acquired by Paco as they drove the large flock west along Paramatta road in a long line.

"You sure about this trip?" Carmen asked as she admired the large Brumby horse that Mel had acquired, and he explained about the shaggy beast. The two other pack horses he had bought were also of this wild and sturdy, if shaggy, breed. Mel was admiring the two dozen horses Carmen had shipped from America, wishing he could afford them, but the woman wasn't selling anyway, as was attested by the many offers she had received and turned down for the fine beasts. Still, Mel had put in for one of their offspring when they became available, knowing his new friend would hold it for him even if it was years in the making.

"Nope, I'm not sure about this trip, but I'm willing to look wherever my heart is sending me," she replied cryptically.

Carmen had figured out Mel's secret after their first week on the trip. She understood the large woman's need to keep her identity under wraps and didn't pry. She respected her too much to reveal her secret. She let on to Mel that she knew, but from the little she had gleaned about being shanghaied and ostracized by her peers back in New England, she thought she understood why Mel would rather go about as a man. She certainly had more freedom as a man; the transaction at the bank had proven that. She also sensed Mel's attraction to her, and while it pleased her vanity, the feeling wasn't returned.

Mel had been pleased to meet Carmen's children. The maturity of the four children was a surprise as they occasionally rode along on horses belonging to their mother, not in the least afraid of their size.

They also weren't fearful of Dancer, the stallion that Carmen rode. She didn't ride side saddle, and they were well supplied with western saddles, one of which Mel purchased. She didn't like that the Australian saddles had no pommels, and she felt more comfortable in the familiar Western one.

They continued west on the track they were assured would take them to Menindee. They had to cross a river there that some described as being so muddy that the good water ran under all the silt. They said it ran upside down, and Carmen had appreciated the humor of that. Used to the clean waters of the Sierra Nevada mountains in California, she missed the cold, clear water. She'd enjoyed the Blue Mountains here in New South Wales as they traveled through them but was told that wasn't even a quarter of the trip on their journey to Twin Station.

Carmen had a lot to think about on this trip, like meeting Mel Lawrence, the American who had assured her she had been shanghaied. Mel had confided in her but only after Carmen had accidentally discovered her secret. Mel Lawrence was not a big-boned, burly man but a big-boned, burly woman. Melissa Lawrence had mistakenly been taken for a man because of her short hair, mannish attire, and her size. Not willing to be gang-raped on the vessel that had absconded with her person, she let them think she was a man, hiding her sexuality from them in the months it had taken to cross the vast ocean from San Francisco. Working hard, they didn't suspect the large person was a woman and accepted her at face value as a man. Carmen realized now that her own vessel transporting her worldly goods, horses, and people had left many months apart from the ship that had taken Mel.

Mel had also asked that Carmen keep her secret, which she willingly agreed to. She knew there was probably a good reason for it and hoped to someday find out. The two Americans had become good friends in this foreign land while both heading for the Outback.

CHAPTER TEN

As they were coming out of the Blue Mountains, heading for Bathurst and then past it onto the rolling hills, they encountered drays pulled by bullocks bringing back mounds of wool from the various stations. This group of men were a cordial lot and anxious to get back to Sydney, but one of them stood out because he owned an aboriginal woman. Camping near them, they were able to listen to the boisterous talk and bragging of a few of the men, who were intent on impressing the Yanks. A few tried to flirt with the Senora, not in the least intimidated by the vaqueros she had with her. The big Yank backed up the vaqueros, and a few of them men backed down. They didn't realize that the Hispanic men were more of a threat while protecting their Senora.

The men were interested in the large flock of sheep the Americans were taking onto the Outback and exchanged information. Mel was watching how the carter treated the woman in his care and decided to challenge the men to a game of cards. She played to their vanities and finally enticed the one named Bradley, who apparently owned the woman, to play cards. She didn't even have to use the tricks she had learned so long ago in New Orleans to win against the man. His confidence, ego, and overweening pride kept him in the game. Mel let him think he was a good player, keeping him in the game just long enough for him to borrow against the woman's value and then lose. Mel had to get a little forceful to collect her bet, but the man sulkily complied eventually and turned the woman over to the big Yank.

"What are you going to do with her?" Carmen asked Mel, referring to the chained Australian Aborigine she had acquired.

"Free her," Mel said shortly and succinctly. It had never occurred to her to keep the woman. She looked distastefully at the collar around the woman's neck and the chain attached to it. The chains around the woman's ankles were equally alarming.

Carmen nodded, never doubting her friend or her decision to acquire the woman. The woman looked afraid, ready to bolt, but Mel tried to lessen her fear by communicating with her.

"Dog…daaawg," she said, drawing it out and pointing at the dogs as they came in to eat.

The woman tried. She realized her new man expected her to learn his language, but some sounds, no matter how hard she tried, were difficult for her. Still, she was eager to learn as she realized that being able to communicate with these white men would be a good thing. She was surprised that they were heading back the way she had come. The wagons—way-guns, the man told her—were heading back towards the Outback. She wondered if she could get back to the area where her family was. Then she realized, her family would never accept her. Her father had abandoned her because her value was gone. Realizing her family was forever gone to her, she decided to make the best of what was before her. The man was kindly to her and teaching her his white words. She looked about more now, not forced to look down while trying to avoid being noticed by the men. No more was she used, and Mel had supplied her with more clothing.

Carmen watched as her friend attempted to teach the aboriginal woman, her patience tested as the intelligent but rather primitive woman was at first fearful and then, seemed to learn by leaps and bounds. Carmen was fascinated watching the two women interact. She was pleased to see the Aborigine seemed to enjoy her children, who were equally fascinated by the woman whose name they all learned was Alinta.

They stopped in the next town, and Mel sought out a blacksmith to remove the collar and chain, selling the metal back to the man. Mel looked on curiously as the blacksmith removed the restraints, not having seen a slave collar before, and realizing the only way to remove it was by sheer force.

Alinta struggled at first, not having understood when it was first being put on, and now, not willing to have another put on. Carmen watched when Mel firmly held the wild woman as the man removed it, the wool between the collar and her neck falling away. The Hispanic woman watched as Alinta felt wonderingly at her neck when Mel put her back on her feet and smiled at her. The collar, despite the wool padding, had chafed, and Alinta must have felt the loss of weight immediately from the heavy iron. She was equally surprised when the man removed the manacles around her ankles. She looked at the despised collar and watched as Mel offered the metal to the other man, who negotiated for the used iron, a commodity he could well use in his blacksmith shop.

Next, Mel and Carmen headed for a store. Those inside frowned as the Aborigine entered with them but shut their mouths as Mel quickly looked for ready-made clothing and paid for it with cash. Mel's size alone kept them from ordering the aboriginal woman out of their store. Carmen wasn't aware when the frowns were directed to her own darkly tanned skin, but when she mentioned she was going out to Twin Station and was one of the owners, their attitudes changed, although, they were still doubtful. Alinta didn't understand at first when Mel held up first one shirt and then another against her body to see if they would fit, followed by miner's pants and underwear. A small, almost childlike stockman's hat completed the outfit, and Alinta carried it all, not understanding it was for her to keep. As Mel and Carmen headed back to their camp outside of the small town, Alinta followed, hurrying to keep up with the taller woman's long strides.

Carmen nodded encouragingly, pleased at the large American's actions towards the poor woman and wondering what Mel would do for her next. She could see the Aborigine was confused by turns and wondered when the woman would realize Mel was a woman too. She watched as the woman learned to wear clothing, although she wouldn't use everything that Mel had supplied her with. She preferred less clothing, and as they saw other less civilized Aborigines than the ones in Sydney, Carmen understood. It was simply too hot for a lot of clothing. She was sweltering in her clothing, and it continued to get hotter the farther west they traveled. The children complained, their nurses complained, and her men were stoically quiet about the heat. It had been hot in the inland valley, but this was a different heat. It was dryer and dustier, and she worried about her horses and how they would adapt to this land. Still, she loved watching them in their herd off to the side of the trail the sheep and their wagons traveled on. They would occasionally run, their manes and tails flowing in the wind and their beauty obvious to all who watched.

Carmen observed that Mel allowed the aboriginal woman other freedoms. Her gathering stick had been lost when she was captured, and Alinta had searched among the deadfalls for another that she could fashion, using stones to smooth it and create another. Mel watched, wishing she could ask the Aborigine what she was doing. Still, the word game, as Mel termed it, was coming along, and Alinta had a phenomenal memory. Carmen and her children participated, taking great delight in the game. Alinta remembered all the words she had acquired, only having to repeat them two or three times before they were hers, so long as she understood the concept. Mel was surprised that the woman had no words for dog or horse in her own language. Apparently, they didn't have these animals where she came from. The closest she came to dog was dingo and that seemed universal. They heard the wild dogs, usually at night as they trailed their large flock for a time, but the combination of man's smell and dogs seemed to be a deterrent. However, while they were traveling, they entered other territories where more of the wild dogs existed and tried their patience by attempting to make a meal of their sheep.

Alinta took an interest in their cooking too, amazed at the bounty that was in their wagons. The rice and peas were a favorite of hers, but she didn't really like the fat from the mutton, preferring the meat to be nearly raw rather than well done. Salt pork gave her a taste that left her in awe, and beef was her favorite meat. She searched for and found seeds and other things off the trail as Mel allowed her to roam, only worrying once or twice that she had run off.

"She'll have to go eventually, won't she?" Carmen asked as they rode their horses at the front of the column, the dust that the sheep kicked up on the track too thick to ride drag very often. She glanced back to see the flock going on endlessly behind the wagons on the track. Her other glance took in the two men assigned to their remuda, the horses being herded alongside their long column were moving much faster than the slower wagons and sheep, who were permitted to graze as they went.

"I hope she will be happy to be returned to her family," Mel said, watching the aboriginal woman effortlessly club a lizard and put it into the bag she had given her. Carmen had watched Alinta, who was amazed at the fine bag, much finer than any she could have woven from spinifex. She had turned it over and over after Mel gave it to her, examining it closely.

"You think they will want her back?" Carmen asked knowingly, comparing the Aborigine to the native Indians she had known and dealt with in California.

"I have no idea. That's one thing I hope to ask her as she learns English." Mel did worry. The woman, almost a girl, seemed cheerful, well-meaning, and bright. Did she want to go back to her family? There were many things she wanted to ask her, but the language barrier was only part of the problem. The woman didn't seem to have what Mel would have termed common sense. She didn't seem to understand that things could be broken and everything wasn't made of iron. Alinta had cringed in terror when she accidentally broke a bottle and their cook, one of Carmen's men, had started yelling in consternation over the broken glass. The rapid phrases in Spanish had sounded musical, but the tone had frightened the wild woman.

"Easy there, easy. It can be replaced, right, Jose?" Mel asked as she came running up where Alinta cowered, expecting a blow to fall. She pulled the girl up and into her arms. She towered over her at least a foot, and her heart went out to the terrified girl. Carmen came rushing up, talking rapidly to Jose as Mel asked him.

"Si, si," he said contritely, upset and swearing over the mess of the glass in his carefully prepared food. He began shoveling it into the fire. No one could eat food that had glass in it. "I am sorry, Alinta," he said, trying to touch her on the arm as she cringed away. His face told how sorry he was as he watched her.

Alinta might not understand the words, but the tone told a lot more, and his body language gave away a lot more than he intended. She looked at him wonderingly, understanding him as little clues gave her ideas about what was being said. She realized that Mel was holding her but not so hard that she couldn't get away if she wanted. She looked up at the big man with as much wonder as she had looked at Jose, then glanced at a concerned Carmen. Realizing no one was angry at her and no one was going to strike her, she relaxed. Hearing the concern in Mel's voice towards the man named Jose, she began to fit these things together in her mind. Things had changed a lot for this primitive woman, and she was trying to figure out these white people.

Alinta could see that Mel and Carmen were vastly different white people, and although the Hispanic people were dark too and getting darker from the hot Australian sun, they were still a lot lighter than her own people. She didn't think of them as Hispanic because that concept hadn't been explained to her, but at the same time, she wouldn't have understood it yet either. Mel was obviously one of those white men but nothing like the ones who had captured her. His kindness alone intrigued the aboriginal woman.

"Did Alinta do something bad?" Rachel, Carmen's young daughter asked worriedly as she came running up, her nurse a few paces behind her.

"No, it was an accident," Mel explained to the little girl, her voice softening.

Alinta was fascinated by Carmen's children, not having seen white children this close before. The children she had seen in the towns they had gone through, some which she had seen again as they retraced the previous route, never came near the wild woman. The offering of friendship between the town's children and the travelers, even if only temporary for an evening, was immediately accepted, and she watched avidly as they played together.

Alinta left the safety of Mel's arms to help Jose. He was at first surprised by her attempts to help him clean up, then she cut herself on the glass, not understanding that it was sharp and the shards dangerous.

"She's bleeding. Alinta's bleeding!" Rachel announced upon seeing the blood as she watched the adults interact.

Alinta put her thumb wonderingly in her mouth, tasting the food, the dirt, and the blood on it immediately and spitting it out.

Mel gently pulled her thumb out of her mouth and handed her a handkerchief, which she showed her how to wrap around the bleeding thumb. The red color of the material seemed to fascinate the woman as she stared at it. Mel applied pressure, amused at the primitive woman's fascination and wondering what would happen to her when they parted ways. She too had noticed the rounding belly and knew it wasn't just from their good food. She felt strangely maternal towards the woman, but at the same time, she knew she cared deeply for her and worried what would happen when they found more Aborigines and Alinta went with them.

Carmen wondered if Mel was aware that she was falling for Alinta. She found it fascinating to watch and observe. She attempted to help where she could, but she could see that Alinta wasn't aware of her dependence on the big American yet either. She wondered how crushed Mel would be to lose her pet or if Alinta would even go.

CHAPTER ELEVEN

They traveled steadily to the west, and it got hotter and hotter. They tried to stop near a pond, a billabong as they called it here in Australia, whenever they could. Creeks and streams were not plentiful here, but the farther west they went, the less water there would be. Carmen remembered that many parts of California were like this and yet, the feel of the Outback was completely different. It was older and more oppressive than anything she had ever felt before.

As their large flock and contingent paused at the top of a hill that led down to a large river, their guide announced it was Menindee. He pointed to the track that was visible on the opposite side of the river. Carmen thought it atypical of a western town, being dry, dusty, and raw. There were streets, but they weren't tree-lined or cobbled as had they would have been in a more settled city like Sydney or San Francisco.

"You'll have to arrange for the ferry to take your sheep across, missus," he addressed Carmen since she was going to the station where he was taking these supplies. He didn't trust the men who rode with her, but an attractive woman always seemed to garner compliments along with flirtation and respect. He grudgingly respected the big man who frequently rode with her, the other Yank, but only because he had heard of the one punch knockout in the shearing sheds back in Sydney. He'd eyed the man several times but knew better than to start anything with him. The big American was curious about everything and frequently asked about animals, birds, and even grasses and trees they encountered. Carmen listened as well, learning the names. His men kept well away from the big man for the most part, just in case they unintentionally offended him.

Carmen and her people kept to themselves, not socializing as the Australian and English men found the Hispanic Californios very different. Even Mel, who they continued to call a Yank, was like the swarthy men from the southwest part of the United States, and the Australians eyed them suspiciously. Carmen and her men were used to this back in America, which was still young, but their people had been in California for hundreds of years and here they were the newcomers.

Mel was grateful that the vaqueros were willing to help with the sheep; they weren't stock snobs as she had seen in the west. Some cattlemen wouldn't associate with sheep ranchers and vice versa. She'd known it to come to violence. Here it seemed to be reversed. Sheep were much more numerous than cattle, and while she hoped to also obtain some beef, right now, her focus was on the sheep she had purchased with Carmen.

"We'll do that," Carmen said, giving the blushing man a smile as she nodded in agreement.

"Can't we swim them across?" Mel asked, eyeing the dirty river and trying to gauge its depth. They'd swum the flock across many nameless creeks on the trek out here.

"No, sir. It's deeper than it looks," the man explained respectfully, trying to stop from blushing in the presence of a beautiful woman and having to talk to Carmen. The drayage company would pay to ferry his wagons across too.

They stopped in the town to pick up a few odds and ends, and Mel arranged to load the sheep on the ferry in batches, so they could take them across the large river. Leaving some of the dogs on the other side with a couple of the men, the ferry returned to take more and more of the sheep before taking the wagons and people across. Carmen was amused watching Mel, knowing that the men who did business with the Yank had no idea they were dealing with a woman. They ignored Carmen for the most part, only talking to the big Yank they assumed was a man. Other than curious stares, admiration for her dusky looks, and an odd 'G'day' here and there, most of the men they dealt with didn't talk to the Californian.

"Someday, they will have steel rails leading to towns such as this," Mel commented, looking back as the town receded across the river.

"I hope it doesn't ruin the land," Carmen agreed as she imagined it. She knew since California had become a state in 1850, men had already been talking about the steel rails running from one end of the country to the next. With the changes that had already threatened her family ranch and her sale and emigration, she could imagine the fights, the influx of less than desirable men and women, and the crime that would increase once it was finished. She wasn't to know it, but it wouldn't happen in the United States for many years. The railroad wouldn't be complete until 1869 with the Transcontinental Railroad.

They rode on along the track, stopping every third day or so, so the sheep could graze and maintain their weight.

"This country is larger than I had given it credit for. No wonder my letters to my cousins and uncle took so long to be answered," Carmen confided as they rode along.

"Mama do you think I could ride today?" one of the boys called from the back of the wagon where he rode with his brothers, sister, and nursemaid. This nursemaid looked exhausted from taking care of the four children.

"Don't you think it's too hot?" Carmen answered, looking at the sweat that dripped down the boy's face. She herself felt the same way and frequently used her delicate handkerchief to wipe away the dust and sweat from her face. The handkerchief was no longer a pristine white lace. She had drawers filled with these feminine fripperies, and she was glad she had stopped wearing her dresses and now wore the stockmen's clothes that Mel had recommended she purchase back in Sydney.

"No, Mama. I think being on the back of a horse will be cooler than sitting here in the wagon. If there is any breeze, I think I will feel it better there," Philippe insisted logically.

Carmen shared a smile with Mel. The boy would ride every day if he could. Neither of the women felt the aches in their legs anymore. They had worked them out before they had even crossed the Blue

Mountains back near the coast. The boy tried to ride for several hours a day and had built up his stamina each time.

"Okay, when we stop for the nooning, you can saddle one of the horses for you and your brother," she indicated Sebastián, who was sitting behind him looking hopeful.

"But, Mama, I wanted to ride alone," he protested, not liking the idea of sharing.

"Then perhaps, you don't need to ride at all."

He thought about it for only a second, not willing to lose the chance to ride instead of being stuck in the wagon with his younger siblings. "He can ride with me," he conceded.

"He won't last long," she assured him with a smile, and she and Mel rode on ahead of the wagon. They had only stopped back by the wagons to be assured that Alinta was riding in one after having caught her foot on a thorn.

"Wish I could get her to wear shoes or boots," Mel groused as they checked on her, and she smiled, pleased to see the Yank.

"Are you trying to civilize her?" Carmen questioned, amused. She remembered hearing of whites trying to do this to American Indians…and failing.

"No, not at all," Mel shook her head. "I just want her to be comfortable…" she began and then left off. "Hell, she was probably comfortable with no clothes for generations." They'd seen a few *wild* Aborigines as they headed west, each time making Mel worry that Alinta would take off and go with them. So far, though, she hadn't seemed to want to go with any of them even though they looked at her curiously. She was still wearing the long, white man's shirt…and that was it. The clothes that Mel had bought for her were rolled up with her

bedroll and becoming all wrinkled. The hat was her one concession, and she wore it proudly.

"Thinking we can change the natives has caused more problems than anything else. My ancestors were conquistadors, and look how well that turned out," Carmen mentioned, remembering the stories of the Spanish who came over and took over Mexico, killing thousands of natives, breeding with them, and trying to conquer them. Eventually, they had civilized some and taken some as their wives, but they were far different from the original Spanish men and women their ancestors had been. Even the Californios she had known were different from those who visited from Mexico or Spain. They were becoming Americanized, and she wasn't sure that was a good thing. Still, she didn't regret leaving and was looking forward to seeing Twin Station and her inheritance.

"You've been on Twin Station for a day now," the carter told her one day as they traveled. They had been on the track for months because of the sheep slowing them down considerably, and he could have left them behind, but because she was one of the owners, he had instead stayed with them. Carmen appreciated it.

"When will we be at the home paddock?" she asked, looking about the land now with a proprietorial air. She found it dry and dusty, very much like the desert.

"Tomorrow," he promised, calling to one of his men to go on ahead and warn them. Carmen looked nothing like the Englishman, but she stated her uncle had been English, and he had known the man. If she had made the whole story up, then why would she travel this far with all these animals for nothing? She had to have money in order to transport those horses, her people, and all this baggage from the

Americas, much less purchase those sheep. He knew that the big Yank owned half the sheep, but he didn't know why they were traveling together. He had gleaned from the campfire talk that the Yank was going to look for his own station nearby Twin Station.

CHAPTER TWELVE

Carmen was restless that last night, wondering what they would find at the station tomorrow. The children were excited, the end of their long and grueling trip ahead of them. They'd talked about what they wanted in a home, speculating what they would find, and remembering the ranch house back in California. Nicolás already had fading memories, and Rachel wouldn't remember the ranch at all, but they both acted up because their older brothers were excited.

The land looked arid, and as they came over the last rise, Mel rode ahead to direct the sheep away from a flock she saw grazing on the hillside. They were at least half a mile away, but if two flocks came into the vicinity of each other they would flow together, their herding instinct mandating it. She didn't worry about separating her part of the flock from Carmen's when she left, but she wanted the breed she had paid for, not the sheep she'd seen grazing on the stations on their way out here. Carmen had already agreed to give her three- and four-year-olds from the flock. These would help establish her station quicker as the animals were more likely to give birth to twins or more at that age.

Two people came riding down the track. As they got closer, they saw it was a man and a woman, and Mel nodded to acknowledge them as she also watched the oncoming wagons and sheep. Carmen saw them too and rode up just as they reached her.

"Are you Carmen Pearson?" the man asked, eyeing Mel.

"I am Senora Mary Carmen Valenzuela Pearson," Carmen said with a flourish in her voice as she reined up. "You may call me Carmen."

"Ah, cousin Carmen," the man said with a bright smile, relieved that the pretty woman was his cousin and not the other…woman? He was curious and then realized it was a man…or was it? He eyed Mel and then looked back at his cousin. "I am Harold Polaski, and this is my sister, Fabiola."

At the names, Carmen's perfectly sculpted eyebrow raised.

"I know, most people don't expect such a name," Harold explained. "I believe your uncle may have had a hand in influencing the name of my sister," he said with a smile, trying to be charming.

"This is Mel Lawrence, who is traveling with us," Carmen introduced her traveling companion, and Mel nodded.

Harold looked at him again, trying to figure out if he was a man or a woman. Fabiola nodded coldly, looking every inch the landowner…strong and capable. Harold looked, well, weak. His boyish good looks were fading as he grew older. Used to being indulged a bit as he grew up, he could appear the eligible station owner but failed to maintain that facade for too long, as they would soon learn. "We were wondering when you would get here, but we never expected you to bring stock." He looked beyond her at the sight of the eight thousand sheep, the herd of horses, and the wagons. He looked…alarmed. "We do have sheep here," he pointed out.

"Half of these belong to Mr. Lawrence," Carmen explained, gesturing to Mel.

Mister. That meant that he was a man, not a woman as Harold had wondered. Fabiola looked on, not saying much as she watched the strangers and the stock they had brought with them.

"I also thought that having Merinos in our breeding would be good for wool production," Carmen continued, echoing almost verbatim a conversation she had had with Mel many times on the trip out here and explaining why she had immediately set out to obtain the sheep when she found them. Mel had repeated what she had learned of breeds, having listened to Foster and his men as well as other station owners and grazers she met. Carmen had previously raised beef and horses but not sheep. She had relatives who were sheep herders but hadn't a lot of experience with them herself. She had learned a lot on the trip out here as Mel willingly shared what she had learned.

"Then you will be staying?" Fabiola spoke up, sounding haughty.

"Yes, I sold my ranch in California to come here. I take it you didn't get my lawyer's letters?" Carmen asked, feeling equally haughty towards the woman.

"Yes, we got your letters, but did you get our letters asking if you would be interested in us buying you out?"

"I wanted to see what I had inherited," her arm swept out to encompass the immense landscape around them, ignoring the question. Of course, she had gotten the letters, dealt with the lawyers, and

decided against selling. Her eyes didn't betray her thoughts, and she wondered if something was not as it seemed with her cousins.

The first of the wagons had passed by them, and the sheep were coming up. Mel moved away to help keep the sheep away from the flock that was moving away. She whistled to her dogs to keep them on the side away from the other flock, herding them well away. Both Harold and Fabiola watched this.

"That's a lot of Merinos," Fabiola commented, her face relaxing as she talked about the stock.

"We were lucky. They'd just come off a ship and were confiscated by the bank. Mel there recognized them for what they were, and we bought them."

"Is he your partner too?" Harold asked, puzzled, wondering at the relationship and frowning. He'd tried to remain optimistic about their distant *cousin* coming to live at the station. He had been angry that she wouldn't let them simply buy her out, but Fabiola had shrugged, not caring so long as they could stay on the ranch they had grown up on, and there wasn't much worry in that since they owned half the station.

"No, Mr. Lawrence is planning on setting up his own station, and I had hoped you two would have recommendations of where he should locate it. Perhaps, we could use a neighbor?" she hinted broadly. "In the meantime, do you have the pens to accommodate this flock and my herd?" she indicated the horses.

"Of course," Harold assured her, but Fabiola watched her closely, wondering at the Hispanic woman and why she had given up a ranch in California to come here.

They rode to the top of the rise and looked down on the valley that held the home paddock. It was a wide, large valley with a creek that meandered down the middle. The station house was beside it as well as pens, barns, and sheds. It wasn't an overly large home paddock, they'd seen bigger on the way out, but it would be adequate, if a bit rundown. Carmen looked down on their destination and wondered at its setup, disappointed with how it looked. She hadn't expected a fine house and green pasturage after all the arid land they had driven through, but this was barren. She could see an Aborigine village on one side and what must be the station house on the other. Large barrels were on stilts for water, and the houses were also on stilts to keep out bugs and keep everything above the water level of the creek when it rained.

Harold rode on ahead to get men to help with the sheep. He knew the flock was valuable with those fine Merinos and wondered how set that Lawrence person was on taking half. If he could talk him out of it, he'd be happy. Cousin Carmen was right. The Merinos would be good for increasing their wool production, if they survived. He watched as the men herded them into the paddocks, seeing how well they had traveled. It was then he noticed the Aborigine, several other Hispanic women, and the many children with them. There were also the dozen men that looked swarthy to him and the usual carters who brought their supplies. They had been long overdue, and now, he understood the delay was because they had accompanied his cousin out here.

For the first time since they had left Sydney, the sheep and horses were corralled, and both Mel and Carmen breathed a sigh of relief. They'd kept the sheep in rope corrals, folds as they were called here, and only the sheep thought they were safe in them. The folds didn't really keep them contained, but the sheep thought they did, so along with the dozen dogs, the patrolling men, and the guns, it did.

Carmen was welcomed into the main house, a four-room affair with two bedrooms, a front room, and a kitchen. She looked on at the primitive setup without saying anything, but Paco was horrified. After the large hacienda she had left in California, she should come to this…this hovel? He kept his face carefully schooled as Carmen wasn't saying anything. She simply looked around and learned the setup. From what she was seeing, there was no way her cousins could have afforded to pay her the sum they had offered for the station.

"He can sleep in the bunkhouse with the other men although with all your other men…" Harold began hesitantly, referring to Mel.

"My vaqueros?" Carmen corrected gently, giving it the full Spanish flavor as she asked.

"Yes, with your other men," he repeated himself, not even trying to use the Spanish word, "it's going to be a tight fit. The bunkhouse can only hold a dozen."

"What are some of those houses along the creek?" she asked.

"They're for some of our married stockmen…" he began slowly as he realized what she was saying. "Three of them are empty," he offered up half-heartedly. It was obvious he was reluctant to give them out, but Carmen was more than a match for him.

"Mel, you and Alinta can take one of the empty houses there along the creek," she called, taking charge, seeing the large woman walking her horses along and heading for the corrals. The woman nodded and turned to what looked like an empty house.

"Paco, if the bunkhouse is full, use the other empty house for the men," she continued. She turned back to her cousin. "There's that for now until the drayage men return to Sydney."

"They'll go after we unload the supplies and then load the shearing," he explained, gesturing to the various hodgepodge of sheds.

"Yes, that's what they told me," she returned, nodding in agreement to show she understood.

"They're so late," he complained but realized immediately that was the wrong thing to say.

"Yes, that's my fault. I didn't want to run down the sheep or my horses." She turned away, looking into the house and wondering where she and her children would stay.

"Senora, where should we go?" Maria asked as she came up, speaking in Spanish as was her custom.

"For now, let's just get the children settled, so they can go out and play," Carmen returned, gesturing towards the other empty house along the creek. It was obvious she was as comfortable in English as she was in Spanish.

"That's a pretty language," Harold said with a smile, trying to be charming, but it was obvious he didn't like them speaking a language he didn't understand. He watched as the other Hispanic woman began leading the children towards one of the empty houses.

Carmen ignored him, instead watching Fabiola as she got down from her horse near the sheds and started commanding the men who stood around. There was soon activity as they moved about busily. Down by the creek an annoying noise had started. "What is that?" she asked about the noise she heard.

"Sounds like a corroboree starting," Harold explained. "It's an Aborigine celebration. They do it for all sorts of occasions. I'm betting this one is because of your arrival." He smiled, showing even, white teeth.

Carmen nodded and returned the smile, wondering at it and not liking the way the man was hovering. "Jose," she called in English to one of her men, "My things can be unloaded in that house over there," she nodded towards where Maria was heading with her children, another of the nurses hurrying to catch up with them. "Please have the men check on my babies," she added, and he smiled. He saluted her as he hurried away, directing one of the wagons to the house Maria had already disappeared into.

"Your babies?" Harold asked, trying to be amiable.

"My horses," she replied as she walked off the main house porch and headed for the house her children had disappeared into. She found that it had two bedrooms, a living area, and a kitchen. This would be fine for a while, but it wouldn't be big enough for the long-term. "Maria, the men will soon be here with my furniture. Some will have to be stored in the barns until I can figure out what I'm going to do here."

"You will have to warn the children against going under the houses until we've made sure they are clear of spiders and snakes," Harold warned her, proving he had followed her.

Carmen was irked, but she nodded to show she understood and looked at Maria warningly. "Thank you, cousin Harold. I appreciate your concern and consideration," she said sweetly. "We are going to have to discuss with Mr. Lawrence what his plans are and then divide up the supplies he purchased as well as the sheep."

"How keen is he on keeping his half of the sheep?" he asked as Carmen returned to the front porch of the house and looked around. The different angle gave her a better view, and she could see why someone had settled in this area. It must be beautiful after the rains. Right now, it looked parched and dead but still pretty in its own way.

"The sheep were Mr. Lawrence's idea. I have no intention of cheating him out of anything," she informed her cousin frostily.

"No, no. I just thought perhaps he would like to do a trade. Some of our sheep for a share of his Merinos," he amended hastily. Damn, she was prickly and beautiful in her ire.

"We could ask, but I own half that flock, and if four thousand Merinos aren't enough on our station, then how many would be?" she asked.

"Well, all would be welcome, and with them intermixed with our sheep, we should get ahead in a few years."

"A few years?" she turned from where she was observing the activity on the station. "How did you intend to buy me out?"

"Well, over time or with a bank loan," he began feebly.

"I think there is some misunderstanding here, cousin Harold," she began briskly as she saw Fabiola come up. "You don't own this land," she gestured at the hills around the home paddock. "You only have grazing licenses, so you couldn't get a loan on it. From the few sheep I saw on the land while traveling here, I take it you've had some setbacks?"

"We have," Fabiola answered for her brother, drawing Carmen's full attention. She looked hard at the woman. From what her uncle had written, both Fabiola and Harold were the result of his cousin's liaison with an Aborigine. In her cousin Harold's case, he looked white but had a weak chin and characteristics she could see wouldn't serve a white man or an aboriginal man well. In the case of Fabiola, she saw that she was large boned, although not as large as Mel, but totally

feminine in appearance. Her skin tone defined her as an Aborigine, and from what Carmen had experienced herself, she probably would not be welcome in Sydney. People frowned on mixing the races. Even her Spanish heritage was suspect because she and her vaqueros were darker skinned than the English. The Hispanics looked nothing like the aboriginal people in bone structure. "We had fires that wiped out our flocks in the southern paddocks. They were set by fossickers, who were mucking about with no care other than their own. Drought has taken a toll on our remaining flocks, but we are anticipating the rains, and with the influx of your flock we should do better. You're right. We'd never get a loan, and I'm grateful you're here to help. Are your men staying, or are they heading back to the Americas?"

"They're staying," she informed her cousin, impressed despite her first impression of Harold.

"Then they'll be expected to work," she stated.

"Yes, that was the plan. I was uncertain what we'd find here, but I'm willing and able to work," Carmen promised.

Fabiola's eyes sparkled. They had reached an understanding, and she sensed her *cousin* was a similarly strong woman, and she was bred for country such as this. "What kind of station is Mr. Lawrence planning on setting up?"

"I was hoping we might convince Mr. Lawrence to be one of our neighbors, if there is land available and you could recommend something?"

"How about we go out to a few of the paddocks tomorrow. We can take our men some supplies, and I can show you around the place?"

"That would be a good idea," Harold seconded the idea, and Carmen saw the look in Fabiola's eye before she glanced at the brother and back to the tall woman.

"Would you like to rest a few days?" She glanced behind Carmen to where the children were making themselves at home in the house, already running about followed by the faithful Maria and another woman, Gabriella.

"No, I'm used to traveling now. Let's go discuss it with Mel Lawrence and see what…he has to say about it." Her hesitation was only brief, but she wondered if Fabiola had recognized it as her eyes flared slightly.

After Carmen's wagons were unloaded into her chosen house, the rest of her goods placed in some stalls in the barn covered and away from the animals, the Hispanic men pitched in to help unload the rest of the supplies for the station into the storage shed and elsewhere. Fabiola was pleased with the additional help as everyone, including Carmen and Mel, pitched in to not only unload the supply wagons but also stack the large bags of wool, so the wagons of the drayage company could immediately turn around the next day and head back to civilization with their crop.

CHAPTER THIRTEEN

They headed out the next day. Fabiola led the way, followed by Carmen and Mel and several pack horses. Only two of the vaqueros accompanied them to guard the Senora. It had taken Mel several tries before Alinta understood that she was to stay in the house with all the supplies. She had been curious about the place, never having been in one of these structures, but she took the job of *protecting* Mel's things seriously.

Fabiola explained they had split the paddocks into sections to keep track of them, and a stockman oversaw each section, sometimes helped by an assistant, called a jackaroo here in Australia.

Mel and Carmen looked about avidly as Fabiola explained and pointed with her short whip to different features of the landscape.

"My father wanted to enclose all the paddocks, but he was too ambitious, and it never got done. Your uncle enclosed the paddocks to the south before his death, but we ran out of money before we could do more, and those are now gone with the fires."

"This is a lot of land to enclose," Carmen commented.

"It is, but it won't graze as many sheep as it would in, say England. Do they have sheep in America?" she asked, directing her question to both Carmen and Mel.

"Oh, yes, and as it's a new land it too has its problems enclosing large areas to keep the animals contained."

Mel smiled. Carmen was using big words again, and she could tell that Fabiola was a little intimidated, even if she didn't let it show. Fabiola was all bravado on social items but was brilliant when it came to the land and the stock. Mel knew she could learn a lot from Fabiola. Mel and Carmen were both still trying to figure the brother out. He seemed to allow his sister to take the lead. Still, he had stayed behind, ostensibly to supervise at the home paddock while his sister was gone.

She showed them a little valley, which was a bit greener than their own valley where the first flock was located. The dogs didn't bark as they rode into the valley; they were trained not to bark. Instead, they started moving about restlessly to tell the stockman that something or someone was nearby. He looked up and waved when he saw them, curious about the other people with Fabiola.

"John Neighbors, this is Uncle Jude's niece. She's come here all the way from America," she told him, and he nodded. "My cousin, Mrs. Carmen Pearson."

"Aye, we've been waiting on you for a while now," he said with a decided Irish brogue.

"Waiting on me?" Carmen asked.

"News that you weren't going to sell was all over our station. There is little to talk about here," Fabiola explained. "Anything of news about the family or the station owners is news to everyone here."

Carmen nodded, understanding. It had been that way with her people back in the valley since everyone knew everyone and many were distantly related besides. Everyone could count someone related to another person through marriage or kinship. "I'm pleased to meet you," she stated. "This is Mel Lawrence, also of America. He is planning on setting up a station as well."

"How do you do?" John said, holding out his hand to the other man.

Mel shook it, hiding her amusement that the stockman would shake another *man's* hand but not offer to shake the hand of the station owner because she was a woman. She glanced at Carmen and saw that she was also aware of that.

"Where's your hut?" Fabiola asked, not willing to waste time in chin wagging.

He pointed it out to her and saluted as she started off, the two pack horses following her own. He admired the horse that Carmen was riding, but he admired the woman more. Mel was amused when she saw him looking at the beautiful Hispanic woman, but she turned her face away before he could see her amusement and she embarrassed him. He did lose his smile when the two men he hadn't been introduced to glared their resentment as they rode past. He wondered who they were with their short jackets, dark moustaches, and stocky horses.

The camp was set up with a bark hut, obviously not a long-term arrangement. Fabiola got down and the other two helped her measure

out portions of peas, rice, coffee, salt, and other supplies. As they got back on their horses and headed east, she explained that each of the stockmen got an equal share, and she or one of her men visited them once every few weeks to ensure that nothing untoward had happened to them since there were dangers from flood, fire, and wild animals. Each stockman was supplied with a musket and other tools, but their jobs were simply to keep the sheep in good feed and alive. It required moving them every so often, so they didn't eat down to the roots and the graze was kept available and healthy in the paddocks.

"Dingoes are the worst problem, and if you are going into an area where there have never been any sheep, they are going to be a big problem," Fabiola explained, directing her comments to Mel.

Mel nodded. She had expected that and planned for it. She had picked up new guns in Sydney, disappointed that the muskets seemed so old and wishing instead for the repeating rifles she had seen in the Americas. She'd already written to suppliers, but it would take months, maybe years, to get the rifles sent and have them make their way to Australia, if they even made it that far before being stolen.

"I'm planning on shearing my sheep here at Twin Station," Mel explained to Fabiola when she asked about her plans. "We can arrange supplies from here."

"I've already got my suppliers sending me supplies," Fabiola told her, frowning at the wording.

"I mean, if we increase our supplies by sending in larger orders, we can take advantage of quantity discounts and use the same drayage companies that you already have set up. I won't be in a position for a couple of years to have a drayage company haul in supplies and take away my wool clip."

Fabiola nodded, understanding. It was obvious that this man had thought things out, and the fact that Carmen was nodding meant they had to have discussed it. She was surprised how close the two American friends had become but she supposed it was understandable since they were from the same country. She didn't realize how vast America was, just as the two Americans hadn't realized how big Australia was.

They traveled east for hours and came across another stockman. They went through the obligatory introductions again, and Fabiola measured out the supplies. They headed south after that and spent the night with the third stockman, who welcomed the owners and their guests. The variety of visitors provided a welcome respite from the monotony of his existence.

"I heard dingoes last night," he confided. "If someone could watch my flock, I'd hunt those bastards."

"I'll watch them, but I'd rather hunt with you," Mel offered as they sat around the fire, the dogs panting as they lay about between the hut and the fold where the sheep were waiting to be fed. The fold was made up of split rail fencing, and the sheep had settled down inside it.

"You think you could find your way back to the station?" Fabiola asked, looking at Mel speculatively.

"Yep. Your home ranch…er, station is back that way, and as we haven't hit the track that we came in on yet, it must be south and west of here," she said, pointing towards the proper locations.

Fabiola was impressed. The Outback could quickly become disorienting. She was also pleased that Carmen didn't seem to be put out by the vastness of it. "Then why don't you stay and help him?"

She nodded to the stockmen. "If you want, you can catch up with us or meet us back at the station."

Mel agreed and found herself watching the stockmen's sheep the next day as Carmen and Fabiola headed off with the pack horses to supply other stockmen.

CHAPTER FOURTEEN

Fabiola showed Carmen the northeast corner of what they considered their station. "It really isn't marked off because we didn't get the fencing done up here at all. It is more of a feeling," she stated, wondering if the Hispanic woman understood her.

"I see," Carmen mused, glancing at the dip in the land, barely more than a depression. It was certainly not a valley or a gully that she was pointing to. North of them, farther to the west, she could see some odd hills shimmering in the heat as Fabiola pointed out some smoke that signified a campfire and headed for it to deliver more supplies.

As they continued south, Fabiola explained how her father and Carmen's uncle had decided to get as far west as they could from civilization. "I gathered they wanted to see how much land they could take in, then faced with the enormity of it all, they couldn't do as much as they planned. It was too far from civilization, and few men wanted to go with them, despite the promise of steady jobs as stockmen."

"I'm sure it takes a special man," Carmen hesitated a moment, about to add 'or woman' as she included herself and thought about Mel, "to cope with all this."

"The emptiness doesn't bother you?" Fabiola asked, wondering at this cousin who was related to her or her brother very distantly and also by a partnership forged long ago.

"No, my ranch in the California central valley was also remote, although I did have my family about me."

"Your husband didn't come with you?" she questioned, noticing how the Yank had seemed protective of the woman and glancing back at the two vaqueros still following them closely. They helped where they could, but it was obvious they thought their job was to protect the American woman.

"He died several years ago. No loss there," she confided but didn't elaborate. "Some men aren't able to cope with the responsibility of a ranch." Her delicate hand encompassed the land they were riding through and Fabiola nodded. This woman did understand. "How about you? Have you ever been married?" Her uncle's letters hadn't exactly been chatty, and she really knew nothing about her two partners. Uncle Jude had been verbose in his own letters but mostly about Carmen's family—her father and their grandparents—but had only superficially mentioned the children of his partner since they weren't his.

"No man ever took my fancy," she admitted.

"I'm sure there is someone who would give you children?" she asked, feeling that they were exchanging confidences as they got to know one another.

"There hasn't been any I would drop my drawers for," she said with a grin and then turned away to glance at something that caught her attention. Fabiola stared for a moment and then looked away to watch from the corner of eye, but she determined it had only been a wild animal. She glanced down at the gun scabbard on her saddle, confirming the gun was in easy reach if she needed it.

Carmen laughed as was expected, the bluntness something she was becoming used to. These Australians told it like it was, and she liked that. She knew many Americans like that. "And your brother? He has a wife?"

"No, Harold has been looking but hasn't found anyone to his liking." She turned back to Carmen and after studying her a moment asked, "Would you consider marrying again?"

Surprised, she shrugged and shook her head. "I haven't met anyone that has taken my fancy." She thought about the many men she had met on her ranch and on the long journey here. No one had caught her attention in the least. The most fascinating person she'd met that had held her interest had been Mel, and while she knew Mel would have liked if she had shown a romantic interest in the manly woman, she didn't feel that way. Instead, she had been content with a good friendship.

Fabiola watched her cousin surreptitiously, although they were probably both aware of it as they tentatively got to know one another, hoping for friendship or at least a business partnership they could live with. The situation was not one of either's choosing, and they would have to make the best of it.

As they continued onward, Fabiola pointed out features of the station. The wind continued to blow, and endless acres of dry grasses

waved in the breeze. Fabiola pointed out parrots and cockatoos as well as bellbirds and pigeons. Their noises coming from the trees added to the sound of rushing wind through the leaves. Carmen was delighted, having enjoyed the conversations with Mel as the carter had pointed out such things. She loved seeing the odd little koala bears, their jaws grinding up the leaves of the eucalyptus trees. The trees themselves fascinated her with their bark peeling back and exposing the inner tree. Some had very vivid colors. Everything in Australia seemed odd but beautiful to her. Even the snakes, some of which were venomous, had a purpose.

"Avoid boars at all costs," Fabiola cautioned, assuming the American had no knowledge or experience with the wild animals.

"Yes, they told us that on the way out," she informed her. "It reminds me of the javelinas they have in Arizona."

"Javelinas?" she asked, the Spanish word having no meaning to her.

"They too are wild boars."

"Where is Arizona?" She was fascinated as she learned more about this American cousin.

"It is a territory next to California. I have cousins there. This animal sticks mainly to the desert, and its territory extends into Mexico, which is the country south of the United States."

Fabiola shook her head. America didn't make sense to her. "I guess if it doesn't concern our station or paddocks, I have never heard of these places." She grinned wryly; it was all very different, she was sure.

Carmen returned the grin, pleased that Fabiola could admit that about herself. Fabiola wasn't narrow-minded and was willing to hear about the other places, so Carmen shared her own knowledge generously. She could see the beginnings of a friendship forming between them, and it pleased her.

The silence descended upon them, the wind stilled, and the birds stopped speaking. At times like this, the quiet was ominous, and it felt almost as though everyone and everything were waiting for something to happen. It seemed like they were being watched, and yet, there were endless miles of rolling grassland around them with nothing to be seen in the stillness. Both women waited for something to happen, anything. The horses stamped impatiently, sensing the unease of the air around them. The humans exchanged looks, checking if the others were feeling it too and grateful to have the presence of other human beings around them. Then, after this odd moment in time passed, the breeze came back somewhat stronger, the birds started their endless noise, and the leaves on the foliage answered the wind with the sound of their rustling leaves.

"What is it?" Carmen asked quietly after this odd stillness ended.

Fabiola shook her head. "No one knows. It's just part of what makes the Outback unique. Some go mad from being out here," her hand encompassed the plains they were riding through with pockets of forest containing some unique animals. The heat waves shimmered on the horizon. "Others are always a little off, and still, they stay." She glanced at the Hispanic woman, certain she was one of those who would not only stay here but conquer any such matters of the mind and spirit.

They continued their ride eating cheese and biscuits from their saddlebags, so they didn't have to stop. Their only rest was when they searched for and found another stockman and delivered his supplies while he was guarding a flock of sheep.

Carmen reassessed the size of the station time and time again as they rode, acknowledging that she had underestimated it as well as the number of animals it could support. Until the rains came again, the grasses that the sheep and horses could eat was sparse. She could see that in a good year this area might support hundreds of thousands of sheep, but now, the thousands she had brought and the thousands her cousins already had on the station were plenty.

That night, Carmen turned the vegetables in the pan, shaving dried beef into the broth she was making with water. In another pan, Fabiola had mixed damper to make a biscuit to go with their stew. The men returned from hobbling the horses, laying out their bedrolls and using their saddles as a headrest around the fire. The women's bedrolls were on the inside of their little circle and closer to the fire. Carmen could see they were very compatible as she and Fabiola worked to create their supper.

"I would have thought your servants would cook for you," Fabiola commented, ruining the moment.

"Yes, they did, and they do, but I also learned to cook over many a campfire as I took care of my herds of cattle and horses," she mentioned, feeling defensive about the Australian woman's assumptions.

Fabiola realized she had offended the Hispanic woman. She wasn't used to having another woman around. She was usually surrounded only by her own men, her employees, or her brother. Her social skills were badly in need of refining. She changed the subject as they both sat down on logs pulled up near the fire for that purpose. "Do you think Mel will be able to find the home paddock alright?"

"Yes, he should do fine. If anyone was born to fit in out here, it's Mel Lawrence," Carmen answered, smiling as she appreciated the other woman fondly.

"You admire him?"

"Yes, he proved himself on the trip out here and even back in Sydney. He dealt fairly with me on the sheep when I bought half of them. He didn't need to do that. He could have bought them all himself."

Fabiola wondered why he hadn't and thought about that for a while. Not many men would share such a valuable find with anyone else, much less a woman. That showed integrity, and it showed something else. She couldn't put her finger on it now, but she thought perhaps there was more to Mel Lawrence than she knew. She would have to get to know him better.

Their trip was informative and long, and they returned to the home paddock with the supplies well gone. Another one of the men left the next day to finish the rounds on the other side of the station as they had only gone through half of the flocks surrounding their station. The flocks were spread out but not nearly as large as they should be after the losses Twin Station had suffered.

CHAPTER FIFTEEN

The four of them ate dinner together, Carmen and Fabiola discussing where Mel should head to establish her own station. Alinta looked on, not understanding everything they spoke of and surprised at how much these white people spoke and discussed things with each other. While Fabiola would have liked Mel's station to the south where there weren't any of their own flocks since the fire, Mel felt drawn to the north based on conversations with the stockmen they had visited as well as those working at the home paddock.

"I wish to find my own place," Mel asserted. Carmen understood her desire, but Fabiola and her brother, who joined them late in the meal, both tried to convince her that the southern paddocks were empty of sheep and would be to her benefit. "There's more people there too," Fabiola pointed out.

"I appreciate what you are saying," Mel addressed Fabiola and ignored Harold since he didn't contribute much of value to the conversation, just sitting there gazing at Carmen, who also ignored him as she joined in the conversation.

"It wouldn't be like a tenant farmer," Carmen pointed out. "If you go north, you will be totally on your own if something happens. How are you going to deal with Alinta's pregnancy?" she asked, gesturing at the aboriginal woman, who glanced between the conversationalists.

"I guess we will be going slower than I had thought," she admitted. "It will give me a chance to scope out the land and choose where I'll set up my station."

"As far as I know, there are no stations north of here," Fabiola conceded, since the Yank was so determined to go. "East of here there are a few as I'm sure you saw on the tracks, but that is nothing like on the other side of the Cobdogla."

Mel smiled. She loved the Aborigine word for the renamed Darling River, which she only knew because of the endless conversations on the long trip out here. "I expect it to be that way for my lifetime," she agreed. She sounded eminently satisfied with that idea, preferring to be off alone.

They discussed what she should look for and what she would need for her station. Carmen had agreed to keep some of Mel's many supplies here on her station and start up in a couple of months to resupply her and check on their progress. Fabiola raised an eyebrow at this plan, wondering again at the relationship between the Yank and her cousin. As far as she could ascertain, they were merely friends. She'd been surprised that the vaqueros allowed her cousin out of their sight but saw that they trusted the Yank. The others hadn't been pleased by his returning without the Hispanic woman accompanying him. Fabiola had been impressed that her cousin was able to handle herself. She had used a whip and a pistol without flinching as they traveled along. Her bodyguards hadn't been necessary. Their conversations had been about the land. Fabiola explained what they had done in the years since her own father had passed. Her mother had died giving birth to her weak brother. Her father and uncle had both raised the children, teaching them their letters, making sure they spoke and wrote English, and teaching them how to run the station. In due course, the station had grown, but fires and drought had wiped out nearly half of it in a couple seasons. Even now, they were still re-growing their flocks. The death of first, her father, then, her uncle, and last, the fires to the south had been an additional setback to the isolated station.

Now, her cousin was adding this man to their supply route? Fabiola listened as they discussed things that Mel might need or should look for but found herself surprised and appreciative when the Yank and her cousin included her in their conversation. Her advice, since she had lived out here all her life, was invaluable to them.

"But you've never gone that far north?" Mel confirmed with Fabiola. She was ignoring Harold, who was gazing raptly at Carmen and not contributing.

Fabiola shook her head. "There's always been too much work here on the station that needed tending. Why would I go up there when I'm needed here?"

"Curiosity?" Mel asked with a smile, teasing her and pleased when she returned the smile. It was then that Mel saw the real beauty in the half Aborigine, half British woman. She was truly an Australian mix, unique to the Outback.

"Perhaps," she agreed, surprised to find herself smiling back at the Yank and wondering about him once again. She could tell something there wasn't quite right, but she had yet to think it through completely as too many other things were occupying her mind with her cousin's arrival. Thinking Carmen would be manageable and amenable to their plans; Fabiola had been pleasantly surprised when she wasn't. The challenge to be agreeable and work out their differences of opinion in how the station should be run was quite pleasurable. Fabiola and Harold owned half the station, and if they didn't agree, the other half was owned solely by this cousin, who could outvote them. If their plan to have this cousin marry Harold came to fruition that would negate her half vote and then there would be just two votes instead of three. Harold, for the most part, was agreeable to all of Fabiola's plans, letting her run the station as she saw fit, but it had been his idea to get this unknown cousin of theirs to marry him. After meeting Carmen, he was even more enthused by the idea, but he wondered if her cousin was attracted to this Yank?

Fabiola, having gotten to know Carmen better on their trek back to the station, wasn't so sure about the marriage plan anymore. Carmen showed no interest in Harold, despite his making cow eyes at her, which she didn't even seem to acknowledge.

Carmen and Fabiola helped Mel and the men to separate the sheep. They made sure that most of the Merinos she was taking were the three- and four-year-olds they had agreed upon. The men worked quickly and efficiently as they put the new flock into another large corral. The dust swirled up, coating everything and everyone with a fine layer of dirt.

"Do you have an extra side saddle?" Mel asked Fabiola. "I need one for Alinta," he explained. Fabiola led them to one of the many storage sheds, and they searched for and found an old side saddle. Fabiola also found tallow that she handed to the Yank for restoring the leather. Later, she sold Mel a bridle that he also rubbed the tallow in, making the leather supple and ready to use for the aboriginal woman.

Fabiola was surprised at how much time and effort the Yank was making for the Aborigine. She hadn't seen too many white men try like this. He was treating the woman with far more respect than she had seen in a long time. It was interesting to watch and observe as they prepared to leave Twin Station.

Mel saddled one of the Brumbies she had used as a pack horse and taught Alinta how to ride it. She seemed steady, sitting sideways on the horse as Mel patiently showed her how to use the reins on the beast.

Fabiola and Carmen watched as Mel readied her packs on the remaining horses, checking and rechecking the house for their things, whistling to her dogs, and finally, hoisting Alinta onto the waiting horse before gathering up her own reins and stepping into the saddle. Alinta led the remaining pack horses, but fortunately for the unschooled rider, her horse chose to follow Mel's, which made it easier for her to control the beast. They headed for the holding pens where the four thousand sheep Mel was taking were waiting. Carmen, Fabiola, and several of Carmen's men were coming along for the ride to the edge of the station to familiarize Carmen with more of the land she had inherited. Mel appreciated their help as her dogs brought the flock out of the pens and they began their trek. It took two days to get to the edge of the property, or rather, to the edge of the grazing areas that Twin Station claimed.

An odd set of domed hills was at the northernmost line, and Fabiola pointed it out as they pushed the flock to the top of one hill and let the dogs and the sheep slow on the far side. The sheep immediately slowed to graze the long and untouched grasses. "Well, from here you can choose your station," she said as she viewed the land from their vantage point. "I don't know of anyone else claiming the land, but you'll have to fight dingoes, snakes, boars, and the weather. Watch for fires and other things." She wasn't telling the Yank anything he didn't already know, at least nothing they hadn't discussed, but he looked eager to be off. She glanced at the Aborigine, who followed him on her own horse. She noticed the horse was probably stopping because Mel's horse had stopped and not due to the woman's prowess at riding. Alinta looked slightly ill, her protruding stomach making it obvious that she was pregnant. Fabiola wondered if the woman would lose the child with all the traveling Mel planned to do as he scouted the territory he was going to claim.

"I thank you for your advice," Mel said and looked eagerly to the other side of the domed hills, glancing at Carmen with a smile of delight. Before them, as far as any of them knew, was uncharted territory. It was still arid, but soon, the autumn rains would be coming on. The sheep had grown coats in the months it took to get out to the station and soon, they would be giving birth. The rams she had chosen were among them now, but she hoped to keep them separate once her station was established. "I guess this is goodbye," she said to the Hispanic woman, smiling her thanks for the friendship they had shared.

"No, it is merely goodbye for now. I told you, I'll be bringing you some of your supplies. Don't get lost," Carmen teased, a smile on her beautiful face.

Mel looked at her friend's face, wishing for something that had never been there and pleased that the friendship had come about despite her attraction to the woman. She glanced at Fabiola, sensing her admiration for this woman as well. That was a surprise. She had seen Harold looking almost foolishly and hopefully at their cousin, and she knew that Carmen was nothing but polite to the man, not encouraging him in the least. "Well, we will see you then," she said as she gathered her reins and urged her horse forward with Alinta following.

Carmen watched her friend as she followed the large flock of sheep, her dogs doing an excellent job of keeping the sheep moving slowly, so they could graze. She was pleased that she had been able to sell Mel a few of the dogs she had purchased back in Sydney since they worked so well together, and her cousins had more than enough. She'd kept the three best for breeding, but the others had gone with her friend to keep the large flock in order.

"You will see him again," Fabiola promised, glancing at the vaqueros that had accompanied them.

"Of course, I will. Mel is a unique individual and will succeed at anything...he takes on." The hesitation was infinitesimal, but Fabiola noted it. She'd noticed several times when her cousin had hesitated over certain words and wondered if it was the way Hispanics spoke in America, although she didn't think so.

They waited until Mel reached the tree line and turned back to wave to them all, then disappeared into the woods, her sheep appearing beyond the tree line again a while later, mere white specks against the

greenery. They didn't see the two women or their horses again, and it was time to turn back.

Carmen wondered how often it happened in the Outback or in other areas of Australia where some man took a flock or a herd into unchartered wilderness and started anew. Mel certainly wasn't the first, and she wouldn't be the last.

"I'll take you to our northwest border and show you that," Fabiola promised her cousin as they began to make their way off the odd, dome-shaped hills.

CHAPTER SIXTEEN

The ride back didn't seem as long, and it certainly went faster since they didn't have the large flock of sheep to slow them down. Fabiola was proud to show off the station, the various hills, and the valleys encompassing many miles of grazing land. They discussed every aspect of raising sheep they could think of.

"I think we should bring cattle out here too. There are places and land that aren't suitable for sheep," she pointed with her whip, encompassing a valley that had no sheep in it. It was certainly dryer here in the northwest area Fabiola was showing her.

"Someday, we will..." Fabiola began, sounding defensive, as though every hill and valley that showed promise should have sheep on it.

"No, I just think we should diversify, so if another fire or some other calamity should come along, the loss of sheep won't destroy our station," she clarified. "I don't mean to offend."

Fabiola admitted to herself that she resented the interference. She had run the station alone for far too long. Harold was useless. He was just there, overindulged, and merely giving the appearance of running some things. The men indulged this farce, preferring to defer to a man but knowing that Fabiola ran things. Anyone with a brain could see it was Fabiola who controlled the finances, the men, and the running of the station. Now, there was Carmen, and she seemed to have ideas of her own.

They returned to the home paddock before heading out to the southern paddocks to show Fabiola the devastation caused by the fires that had swept through the area. Although Mother Nature had already started to reclaim the wide swaths of destroyed grazing land, it was obvious another rainy season or two would be necessary before all signs of the fire would be invisible, and they could once again send flocks onto this barren land.

"We've got our work cut out for us, haven't we?" Carmen asked Fabiola cheerfully, looking at the acres and acres of dry and burnt land with only superficial new grasses and brush growing again. Some of the trees had survived in the various forests but many more lay charred and ruined, glaringly obvious under the hot, Outback sun. Even the signs of the once lengthy fencing along this southern border was down to ashes, some blown away in the never-ending winds.

Fabiola was learning to like this 'we' that Carmen spoke of. She'd never really had a partner in the unending work that encompassed an operation such as this. Some of her resentment over the fact that

Carmen was bringing change, had ideas of her own, and had a brain, was slipping as she learned more of what Carmen had in mind.

"How soon can a letter be dispatched back east?" Carmen asked as they once again returned to the home station. She'd welcomed the chance to spend time with her children, who were growing so dark under the hot sun while playing in the creek with their distant cousins and even some of the aboriginal children. She smiled at their antics, wishing she could join them. She was going over the accounts, something she could tell that neither Fabiola nor Harold enjoyed. They were haphazard at best.

"We usually send out mail with our supplies," Harold told her, as though a mere woman couldn't understand that. His arrogance wasn't winning him any points with the American.

"Yes, but what if I wanted to send a letter, if I wanted some things to be brought out with our supplies before they came?" she asked, annoyed at his tone.

"We could send a special messenger," Fabiola answered musingly, thinking that there were some things she too would like to order that she hadn't thought of when the drayage company had sent the last load. Waiting until they sheered the sheep and took the wool away again would be a long time to wait for mail. "I need some things too. If you will get your letter or letters ready, we could arrange for someone to head out."

Carmen sat down and wrote using the desk in the main house since her own desk was in storage. She didn't like this main house at all, and the house she lived in with her children was merely adequate. She had some ideas of her own she wanted to implement but without people here to help or the supplies to do it, it would take years to get it accomplished. She wrote her letters.

They watched as the man who had volunteered to post their letters headed out a few days later. He had a second horse loaded with supplies that he could also switch saddles with, increasing his speed marginally as he covered the many miles from the station to civilization.

CHAPTER SEVENTEEN

Loading up the long line of pack horses with the help of her vaqueros, Carmen and Fabiola planned to take these supplies up to Mel, wondering how the other grazer was coping. The winter rains were upon them, and as miserable as it was to ride in the cold rain, they set out to find the Yank.

"Think Mel will succeed?" Fabiola asked as they rode along, making conversation.

"Oh, yes, she..." she trailed off, realizing her mistake and amended, "he has many admirable traits."

"She?" Fabiola pounced, not willing to let Carmen off for her slip of the tongue.

Carmen sighed. "I don't think Mel wants people knowing that," she said, nodding towards the words that had given away her friend's secret.

Fabiola thought for a moment. Several things were fitting into place now as she took in those words. She shrugged. Mel Lawrence's sex was none of her business. The man or woman's gender was not an issue out here when there was work to be done. If Mel wanted to be referred to as he, she would oblige the Yank. She accepted that being male would garner Mel more respect from the men who worked for her at Twin Station as well as any men who would come to work for her.

Carmen, Fabiola, and several stockmen, including some of the vaqueros, followed the path the sheep had taken as they cropped their way across the range. Noting the fine, large, sturdy folds that Mel was building, they could see she was building with permanence in mind. It still took them a while to find the two people and their bulging flock. Now curious about this land after Mel's teasing comments, Fabiola was eager to see this northern range, realizing it might even be better than the Twin Station range.

"Carmen!" Mel greeted her. The dogs had alerted her to the presence of strangers. She didn't think it was dingoes at this time of day, but the dogs had been agitated for a while, alerting her to their presence. She smiled greetings to the men accompanying the two women, greeted Fabiola by name, and glanced at the many pack horses they had brought with them.

"Mel, that is quite a bit of land you've laid out for yourself. Intending to take over all of New South Wales?" Carmen teased after she had greeted her friend.

"I'm still looking for my home paddock," she admitted. "It's hard in this weather." As she said that the rain continued to plunk down on her stockmen's hat and down over her sheepskins. Everyone was wearing similar attire.

"Hello, Alinta," the two women greeted the aboriginal woman, noting how enormously pregnant she now looked as she sat sideways on her horse watching the sheep and wearing a sheepskin coat.

"Misses Carmen, Misses Fabiola," she said in reply, having trouble with the second name as it didn't come easy to her. She'd practiced often since Mel had talked about these two women admiringly.

"Alinta would you mind showing them where to put our supplies in the hut?" Mel asked her, making it her choice, but the eager, young woman immediately set off on her horse, a couple of the men following behind her pulling the pack horses.

"She's gotten so big," Carmen commented when she was out of earshot.

Mel nodded. "I estimate she's due right after the sheep."

"That sounds like a lot of work," Fabiola mentioned, wondering how Mel was going to cope. She knew she wouldn't want to have a flock this big and a pregnant woman to worry about.

"And two of my bitches are pregnant too," she lamented with a laugh at her situation, which was of her own making. She should have held off letting the rams in among her sheep until later, but there was nothing she could have done about Alinta's due date. They were only guessing anyway, having no real idea when the carter had impregnated the poor woman.

Carmen laughed with her, and after a moment, Fabiola joined in. "Do you want me to send some of my men to help?" Carmen asked helpfully.

"You'll have enough with your own flocks to tend to. I knew what the work entailed before I set off on this adventure," Mel reminded her well-meaning friend.

"I'm sure you did," she consoled. "If you need–" she began, but Mel cut her off.

"Thank you."

"Damned independent cuss. We could send a couple–" Fabiola began exasperatedly.

"I know," she returned, sounding just as exasperated.

Carmen shook her head but laughed, so that Fabiola wouldn't get angry. She knew Mel was independent, headstrong, and probably out to prove a point. Still, the land she had chosen was beautiful, and now, with the rains, she appreciated Twin Station even more. It had been brought to life, and the dismal, empty sections south of the station didn't look so bad with the growing grasses. They'd spread out their Merinos between the various flocks, hoping to interbreed them in the coming years as their flocks increased.

The women discussed the various sheep. Mel could speak knowledgeably, having gleaned a lot from Foster and his men as well as the station owners and stockmen they had met on the trip out.

Both women were glad to help bring in the flock of sheep to the nearly finished fold that Mel had been building despite the winter rains. The rope stretched across on two sides, but the sheep were relatively safe. Dinner was a grand affair as they continued talking about stock. Mel further admitted two of her Brumby mares were in foal, probably due to Carmen's fine stallion covering them on the trip out, but fortunately for her, they weren't due for a while. Carmen and Fabiola had a good laugh over the burgeoning increases in Mel's stock, glancing at Alinta as she ponderously walked about, busily washing up after dinner. They would have helped, but the Aborigine had insisted on doing the dishes herself and feeding the dogs as well.

"Just as independent as a Yank I know," Carmen whispered, loud enough that Fabiola heard her, and Mel started to laugh at the dig. She'd complained good-naturedly how Alinta was becoming more assertive as she learned English.

"She has learned to speak her mind when she knows the words," Mel bragged, proud of the woman and her prowess in the language.

Carmen smiled for her friend, realizing that she had fallen in love with the pregnant woman. Fabiola was surprised to see it too. She hadn't thought about it, and now, realizing that Mel was a woman and not the man she had thought her to be, she realized the relationship that might ensue from this unusual woman. It gave her food for thought.

They only stayed two days, helping to finish building the fold and listening to Mel's plans. Mel sent them on their way with a couple of letters in their possession that she had written. They were to be mailed as soon as anyone came to the station with supplies or left to go back to civilization. She had told them she intended to buy more sheep, cattle, and horses, and she would also be hiring a couple of stockmen. "But not until next year or maybe the year after next," she insisted, still wanting her peace and quiet.

Mel waved as they left, noting the empty packsaddles on the extra horses. The two women and a couple vaqueros who knew Mel returned the wave. The stockmen nodded, wondering at the odd man who preferred to be all alone in the far Outback with his woman and large flock. They hadn't been privy to the conversations between the women, knowing their place was not with the station owners.

CHAPTER EIGHTEEN

Several months later, watching as the men industriously sheared the sheep, Carmen worried about her friend far to the north of their station. The two of them were alone, and she wondered if Alinta had given birth to her baby yet. There was just so much that could go wrong. All those sheep, two women, possibly a baby, and no one for miles.

A man and his crew had arrived, and with Fabiola's reluctant agreement he had started on a house for Carmen and her family that was not in the current home paddock but up on one of the hills. The idea hadn't been well-received. Carmen had other ideas that had also been met with resistance, but at least Fabiola was willing to listen and to be reasoned with. Harold was too pig-headed to understand that a woman might have ideas of her own and be able to implement them herself.

"The last of our flocks should be in in the next couple of days," Harold told Carmen, trying to soften her up. He just didn't understand that she wasn't interested in his fine self and his repeated attempts to cozy up to her and show her that he was worthy of her consideration. After all, where else was there a man or a station owner who could match her. He was the perfect choice for her. At least, he thought so.

She nodded, her worry increasing as she searched in vain for her friend, constantly looking north for the tell-tale signs of a flock of sheep coming into the station. She also glanced to where men, those not involved in the shearing of sheep, worked to clear the site on the nearby hill. After the rains had come to their area and she realized that the seemingly innocuous creek that ran through their valley became a raging torrent that flooded out a lot of the area, she knew the house she intended to be built could not be on the plains but must be safely above them on the hills. She knew some of her plans might be impractical. In fact, Fabiola and Harold had tried to dissuade her of the plan to build up there, but she wouldn't be swayed.

"We could use that money to improve–" Harold tried to gripe to Fabiola, who didn't seem to be helping his suit in convincing Carmen to accept his advances. In fact, the money that Carmen was spending really angered him. He saw other uses for that money, but his purposes were far from her own plans to improve the station they all owned.

"Harold, give up," Fabiola advised, pleased that their cousin had seen right through his plans to make her his bride and control her and her money. She could also see by the things that Carmen had put in the stockmen's house just how the American's taste and style were vastly different from their own. Carmen was well educated but didn't hold that over the two of them, and while Fabiola had learned a lot from her own father as well as Uncle Jude, she was fascinated by Carmen and her intelligence. She found herself respecting the American, and as a result, she consulted her as an equal on the station, something they hadn't intended when they first heard that the American would be coming to live there. "She isn't interested in you."

"She just hasn't been here long enough, and we've all been so busy…" he began thoughtfully from where he was sitting on the porch of the main house. He was watching Carmen, always watching her.

Fabiola sighed. First, he was hardly ever busy. She was just grateful that the nearest town was many miles away, and he wouldn't ride for days to go there. She knew if it was closer, he'd be there carousing. The Aborigines' village was off bounds since the elders had threatened him with their primitive but effective spears. He hadn't even tried since Carmen had gotten there, but she wondered what his plans were since she'd been trying to discourage his efforts to charm and court Carmen. Even Fabiola, who hadn't ever been courted, knew that Carmen wasn't interested.

The arrival of the shearers along with a bandy-legged Irishman and his crew, who had answered one of the letters Carmen had sent, suddenly had some of the men, Carmen's mostly, working on the building site.

"We don't need another main house," Harold had complained.

"You may not, but I do," Carmen said sweetly as she worked with Shamus O'Grady and his crew, outlining what she wanted. She ignored her male cousin for the most part, seeing that he did little on the station and wondering when she saw Fabiola working so hard why she tolerated his slothfulness. Later, when she had a moment to discuss it with Fabiola, she chose the site where the men got to work clearing the area for the house that Mr. O'Grady would build as well as additional barns, sheds, and stock areas. Some of the current buildings would still be used of course, but there were many in need of repair. He worked quickly and efficiently until Saturday night came. Then, he insisted on his 'off' night and that he be allowed to indulge. Unfortunately, so long as he had a little alcohol available to him, he frequently snuck some to the work site, but Carmen wasn't to know that until later.

"I'm going to go look for Mel," Carmen said to get away from watching O'Grady's work. It seemed to slow down after he had his binges. "Watch him," she requested of Paco, who seemed to frighten and intimidate the Irishman. Her segundo rolled his eyes but grinned, knowing that his appearance and lack of jocularity scared the man.

"I'll come with you," Fabiola offered, wondering what they would find. Had something happened to their neighbor to the north? She glanced around the busy sheep folds and saw that the extra men waiting for Mel were chipping in to help with the sheep work. They had come in with the shearers, the supplies, and O'Grady's men in answer to letters Mel had written to hire workers.

Fabiola, Carmen, two vaqueros, and five pack horses left the home paddock and headed north at a quick pace, but they could only go so fast.

"You won't get there any faster," Fabiola warned Carmen, amused and concerned.

Carmen laughed, realizing that she had been leaning forward to urge her horse along but was hampered by the pack horses she was pulling. She acknowledged her cousin's admonition and slowed down.

Whatever they found couldn't be changed and ruining a good horse by forcing it to run longer than it could wouldn't help their situation.

As they approached the hills and started to climb the vague path that was forming between the two stations, they saw the large cloud that indicated a flock of sheep. They were relieved to see Mel, Alinta, and a massive flock of Merinos.

"We thought something had happened to you. It's late!" Carmen explained as she took in the enormous flock. "I see you've been busy."

"More than I could have ever dreamed," Mel answered, relieved to see her friends. She looked exhausted. The vaqueros nodded and immediately handed off the pack horses to Alinta before heading to help keep the flock in line.

"You didn't lose any sheep?" Fabiola asked surprised.

"Oh, yes. We lost plenty, but it's these guys," she indicated the baby in Alinta's arms, the puppies visible from the sacks on both sides of Alinta's saddle, and the anxious bitches following at the feet of her horse, "that really made it all worthwhile," she teased.

"Oh, your *baby*," Carmen's voice changed, sounding like she was crooning as she spoke to Alinta. "What did you have? What did you name it?"

"Baby is girl, and Mel name her Ainia (sounds like ah-nee-ah) after Greek Amazon and like my name," Alinta told her proudly.

Carmen and Fabiola looked at a blushing Mel in surprise, and Carmen smiled. "That's lovely," she told the delighted mother. "I'd like to see her when we stop later. Nothing ever felt as good as holding my babies," she reminisced. "Your English," she exclaimed, "has gotten much better!" She complimented the surprised mother, who smiled shyly.

Mel smiled, enjoying the interaction and relieved to see her friends. "Have the shearers left?" she worried as she addressed Fabiola.

"No," the Australian shook her head. "We told them we were waiting on some of our additional flocks and convinced them to stay on. They had a couple of our flocks to do yet, so we should get this flock to them in time. That one was worried about you though," she said, nodding towards a now blushing Carmen.

"You said you'd come in time for the shearers?" she accused, attempting to hide her embarrassment over her concern for her friend.

"I tried, but this was a lot, and I'll admit we need help."

"There are a few men at the station who answered an ad you had someone place for you?" Carmen asked inquiringly. "A couple have their wives with them."

Mel nodded, relieved. She had more letters she wanted to write, and she would do so in the evenings when they finished the drive. She hoped there was mail for her as well as the men who had answered her ads.

They discussed the sheep. Mel was happy to see her friend and her friend's cousin. She was hoping to make Fabiola a friend too. She felt the potential was there but understood that the woman hadn't known how to take her before. Now, with nearly a year behind her, she must understand that all that was between Mel and her cousin was friendship and nothing more.

"Who are the carters?" Mel asked innocently. but both Carmen and Alinta knew the question wasn't as innocent as it sounded.

"Oh, the same ones I use every year. This will probably be the last year that I use them though, as Carmen has found some discrepancies in the books and invoices that they made over the years."

"Would the name Bradley be among any of the men working for them?" Mel glanced in time to see Alinta flinch slightly and then looked at Carmen, who was shaking her head to the negative.

"No, I don't recall any of the men being addressed this way. Why? Is there a problem?" Fabiola asked.

"Well, one of the carters we met on our way out here was named Bradley, and I'll shoot the bugger on sight if he comes anywhere near us again," Mel said in a no-nonsense tone and then dropped the subject.

Fabiola looked startled, exchanging a look with Carmen and then looking back at the big grazer and glancing at the gun she wore on her hip as well as the double-barreled musket that was readily at hand in her scabbard. Looking back at Carmen, she happened to see the pleased expression on Alinta's face before she looked down at her baby.

"Well, these sheep aren't going to get to your home paddock any faster without our help," Mel stated, walking her horse off in another direction and halting their friendly conversation.

Carmen and Fabiola exchanged another look before they too went to help with the large flock. Alinta glanced at the three women and tightened her hold on the reins of the many packhorses she was now holding, managing to cuddle Ainia closer as she urged her horse on. Mel had been a good teacher, and Alinta was no longer frightened of the strange beast because she realized she was in control of it.

That night near the fire, Mel told of the valley she had found far to the north where she intended to make her home station. She discussed the flock and how she and Alinta had coped with the enormous birthing process of the many sheep.

Carmen and Fabiola could both count sheep and realized there had to be over eight thousand young now. The dogs were hard-worked and exhausted from keeping them all in. After they stretched the rope fold that night, the dogs lay down, exhausted and waiting for their tucker before being sent around the flock once again.

The two owners of Twin Station were pleased to see Alinta, who had been riding a horse with a bag containing the pups on each side of her saddle. The dogs wouldn't allow the puppies out of their sight and followed the horse constantly, eagerly waiting for the time they would stop, so the puppies could be let down and nursed and the mothers could clean them and alleviate their anxiety over their welfare. Alinta wore a wrap that kept Ainia tightly to her, so she could easily breastfeed the infant as she rode when it was necessary. Behind Alinta were the horses with all their gear piled on them. Poles for making the temporary folds dragged behind them and the pack horses the vaqueros had given her. Mel helped her down, and the other women helped unpack the horses, so they could be hobbled to graze.

Mel explained how she had chosen the baby's name, naming it after an ancient Amazon woman. She was pleased that Carmen knew the story of the Greek god Achilles and the queen named Penthesiliea in Troy. Together, they explained it to Fabiola, who loved the story. The Amazon woman had been named Ainia, which meant 'swiftness.'

"It sounds like Alinta," Alinta said, pointing to herself, wanting to contribute, "but also that great warrior woman, the Amazon."

Mel looked gaunt. The constant worry of keeping a flock so large intact must have weighed on her. Add the responsibility of Alinta and the baby, and she looked terrible. She had large circles under her brown eyes. That night, in the company of her friends from Twin

Station and with the extra men to help keep watch over the sheep, Mel slept like the dead, catching up on badly needed sleep. But she didn't miss her turn to guard the sheep, getting up early for her shift.

She wondered if the dogs could sense her ease as they too seemed relaxed. She stopped to pet the puppies that Alinta had taken from the bags, so the bitches could cuddle their broods and feed them. Both bitches wiggled their butts in greeting, simulating wagging tails that weren't there. She heard Ainia fussing and Alinta trying to calm her.

"May I take the baby for you?" Mel offered and held out her large hands.

Alinta didn't hesitate. She had fed the baby, but she wouldn't settle down afterwards. She watched as Mel talked softly to the infant as she walked off into the early morning light to make her rounds. Just the presence of humans and their smell kept some predators away. Alinta rose to go in the brush and do her morning absolutions. She was using water more now as she had learned that Mel liked clean. She had observed while Mel washed the baby several times. While Alinta would have rubbed sheep fat on the baby, Mel washed it off. She did allow Alinta to rub the crushed leaves that warded off the constant flies and mosquitos but then, she used them too. Alinta stoked the fire as the vaqueros sleepily woke and rose.

"Good morning," Carmen whispered as she came up to the warmth of the fire to help.

"Good morning," Alinta replied, understanding the greeting now from her months with Mel.

"Where is Ainia?" Carmen asked, having hoped to cuddle some more with the infant like she had before they went to sleep the previous night. Fabiola too had held the baby, if somewhat awkwardly. She'd compared it to a newborn lamb with much resulting hilarity from the women.

"Mel took her to calm baby," she said inaccurately, almost shyly, as she wasn't used to communicating with anyone but Mel.

Carmen smiled, knowing Mel had been good with her children on the long trek out here. She wondered if the American had wanted children of her own and if that would ever have been a possibility. Well, if what she suspected between the American and the Australian Aborigine was true, that baby was as much Mel's as it was Alinta's anyway. Carmen busied herself with helping the woman prepare breakfast, so they could all get on their way. It was still a long way across Twin Station.

As they approached the home paddock, other riders rode out to help with the large flock, splitting it into different corrals, so the shearers could start in on the sheep.

Mel and Alinta took one of the empty stockmen's houses, surprised to see a modern house being built on one of the hills beyond the home paddock. "What's that?" Mel asked Carmen as they watched the shearers effortlessly guide their clippers along a sheep. A good shearer was worth their weight in gold as they quickly and efficiently sheared the sheep. Very little blood was spilled, and the maximum amount of wool was taken from the poor beasts, who accepted their lot without any fanfare as they waited patiently to be released. Only occasionally did a sheep fight back, and these feisty ones made it interesting for those helping to keep the sheep processed…from pushing them into the chute to pushing them out back into the corrals. Many of the sheep then had to seek out their lambs, who had been baahing pitifully while waiting impatiently on their dams. It still amazed the women and even some of the men how quickly a sheep could find its lamb among all of those crying out for their mamas.

"Oh, Carmen didn't like our accommodations," Fabiola said as she came up, hearing Mel asking about the building going on at the hillside. She sounded almost British in her tones; the Australian accent was nearly eliminated as she informed the American with a twinkle in her eye as she looked at Carmen.

Other men had come all the way from Sydney to do the work Carmen had sent for, riding with the carters, who brought their yearly supplies and planning on staying on for months to do the work she had contracted them for. The tone of Fabiola's voice didn't tell Mel whether she was pleased with the building or not.

"I'm going to have to get some buildings built on my place as well," Mel admitted. "Maybe I should talk to them about coming out to where I want my home built."

"They'll be wanting to head back to Sydney when they are done," Fabiola told her, the disparaging note in her voice as she said it giving her opinion of the large city she had never seen. "A couple of them already have the willies from being out here." She'd learned that phrase from Carmen and enjoyed using it.

Carmen and Mel exchanged a look as both understood that feeling. Several of the men on the trip out here had experienced that phenomena but neither of the women. Both had instead embraced the endless lands and the feel of forever in the Outback. Mel had even commented once that leaving her old life behind hadn't been a problem. Instead, she felt that she had been born for this, perhaps bred to it as she helped to herd her flock out to the vast Outback.

Fabiola had introduced the men who answered Mel's ads, and several of them agreed to hire on for a year, possibly more, as she assessed how they worked with the sheep. She also had a stack of mail that had come with the supplies she had ordered.

Carmen discussed with her men about helping her build a track onto her station, so the carts they had brought to carry supplies could be hauled in. She explained what she had already built, what she intended to build, and all her other plans. If any wanted to back out after learning the amount of work she had in the planning, they would have the opportunity now and could return to civilization with the drays that had hauled Twin Station's supplies in and would be taking the shearing back. None did. They were wanting the jobs because Mel promised an honest day's wage for an honest day's work.

"Mr. Lawrence?" an unfamiliar voice addressed Mel. Not used to being addressed this way, she turned in surprise to see a cleric standing there with his bible in hand and his starched white color standing out in contrast to his black robes. He looked at her benevolently. She glanced beyond him to see Carmen looking amused, and Fabiola's eyes were dancing with her own amusement.

"Yes?" she asked, wondering if this was a Catholic priest and how she should address him. There was a hint of something in his accent, not Australian and not properly English either.

"I was wondering what you were planning on doing about the welfare of the child?" he asked, as though he were giving her a blessing of some kind.

Mel frowned, not understanding. "What child?" she asked, sounding stupid.

"Why, the child of your…wife?" he asked, sounding surprised that she didn't know what he was talking about.

Mel chuckled. "I don't have a wife," she said before she could stop herself, and she saw Carmen and Fabiola both turn away in their mirth. She realized that the man of the cloth would think that Alinta was her common-law wife and Ainia was her illegitimate child. Now, he must be thinking the baby was born out of wedlock.

"But the child, it must be saved! It must be baptized!" he protested. "We must not take advantage of these poor savages, who inhabit this land. Their simple minds must be protected and saved." He held up his bible to emphasize saving the masses.

Mel was amused. She had attended many churches over the years. She believed in a higher being, but organized religion was not for her, especially not out here. Saving the aboriginal people, indeed. "Have you ever seen these people in action?" she asked him instead, confusing him. "They are one with the lands here. They don't take anything more than they need from the Earth, and they don't need saving." She realized that last line should not have been added as the man objected immediately and began going on about their poor, lost souls. He blathered on so long that Mel found herself agreeing to having Ainia baptized.

"How in the world did that happen?" she asked Carmen and Fabiola as they walked along. Fabiola was yelling at the men that were loitering, telling them to get back to work.

"He wears you down. He's almost as bad as the priests back in California at the missions. They are forever saving the savages, as they

call them." She had seen him come in on the drays, and the men who had brought out their supplies were not thrilled with his companionship as it cut down on their drinking and talking. They had to curb their cussing in the holy man's presence.

"Well, I better go explain to Alinta, so he doesn't frighten her. I've also got about a dozen letters to write," she sighed, remembering the pile of letters she had gone through.

"We should be done tomorrow with your flock," Fabiola reminded her, glancing at the men and the sheep they were shearing, then at the many carts the men were filling.

"Oh, that means they will be going soon," Carmen said, obviously enjoying their visit.

"Well, I do have a station to establish," Mel reminded her friend fondly. She'd been thinking of nothing but her future station since they got here and saw Fabiola's setup. Already, Carmen's influence was obvious in the operations of this station and not just in the building of the house on the side of the hill. Carmen had explained that it was higher up and out of the path of the creek that had flooded so during the rains. She felt that the hill should protect her home from the worst of the winds. She also loved its view.

CHAPTER NINETEEN

The marriage of Alinta, a woman of Aborigine descent, to Mel (Melissa) Lawrence from America was performed in the open air of the home paddocks at Twin Station. The sheep were shorn, and the men were packing the bags onto carts to transport them to Sydney. Those in attendance were pleased to witness the event. Very few realized the importance of the event or the sex of one of the participants.

"Do you, Mel Lawrence..." the cleric droned, having asked for a middle name that Mel did not supply, "take Alinta..." he hesitated over the fact that the woman had no middle or last name. Alinta had given him the name of her tribe, but he couldn't pronounce it, and in his arrogant, white male way, he simply ignored it. He had gotten what he wanted, marriage between these two sinners—it was obvious they had been fornicating since the woman was holding the results of their sins in her arms. He had no idea that the child was not biologically Mel's child or that she was a woman. Only four people attending the ceremony knew this, and they weren't telling, "to be your lawfully wedded wife? To have and to hold from this day forward? For better, for worse, for richer, for poorer? In sickness and in health? To love, cherish, and honor above all others till death do you part, according to God's holy law?"

"I do," Mel said clearly. She was holding Alinta's hands firmly, looking down at the woman earnestly. They were both dressed nicely. Mel had pulled out one of her suits, which was tighter in the shoulders and looser around the middle now. She had given Alinta her only dress, which she then pinned in for the occasion. It swam on the shorter woman but looked like a summery gown.

"Do you, Alinta take Mel Lawrence to be your lawfully wedded husband? To have and to hold from this day forward? For better, for worse, for richer, for poorer? In sickness and in health? To love, cherish, and obey till death do you part, according to God's holy law?"

Alinta had been ready to say yes. She had been nodding after each thing the man said, and she had understood all the words, but he hadn't stopped. He kept adding more words. Only the fact that Mel had agreed to almost all the same words had her waiting before answering in a small voice, "Yes."

"You are supposed to say, I do," he told her condescendingly. He didn't see Mel stiffen at the tone in his voice but Alinta did, and she quickly said, "I do." She didn't know why Mel was suddenly angry. Maybe she was mad at Alinta for not knowing the right way to respond. But Mel was once again smiling down at her brilliantly as the man continued his nonsense words and finally proclaimed them to be, "man and wife." Then, he gave his permission for Mel to kiss her. Alinta blushed as the white woman leaned down and gave her a peck on the mouth in front of all the witnesses, many of them whistling and clapping.

The wedding was immediately followed by the baptism of Ainia, who was given a second name and then a third.

"I baptize thee Ainia Mary Lawrence," the clergyman said, pleased that he could perform this small ceremony for them. He had blessed the water, so it was holy, and he poured the holy water on the child's head, expecting her to cry. Instead, to the amazement of those watching, the child giggled. Mel laughed, and Alinta smiled, but the clergyman was horrified. He had never heard of such a thing. The crying was supposed to signify the bad spirits and the devil leaving a purified child's body, but instead, this child laughed. He stared in horror at the child of mixed races.

As Mel and Alinta turned away to accept congratulations from those attending, Alinta was surprised to be embraced by the women and kissed on the lips by the men. She didn't like that and would have bolted but for Mel's hand firmly holding her own and Ainia held in her arms.

Mel saw the Aborigines from the small village watching on, some knowingly, and she nodded towards them respectfully, especially the elders, who returned her nod of respect. She had spoken to a few who spoke English and told them they would be welcome at her station too, if they so desired. She would need workers, and if they knew of others, they should come see the station she was going to build.

Mel couldn't believe how much the documents the clergyman filled out meant to her. Seeing her name on the marriage certificate meant as much to her as seeing the baptismal certificate. She rolled them up carefully, tying them with a ribbon and planning to tuck them away with her other important papers.

"Well, you did it," Carmen said knowingly, leaning up to pull Mel down for a kiss on the cheek. "I hope you will both be very happy.

"I hope we will be too. Thank you," she told her friend.

Fabiola wasn't as friendly, but she too told the large woman that she hoped she would be happy. "I'm glad you decided on that land north of us. If I had known about your valley, maybe I would have expanded up there, although that would certainly be a huge station. I'd rather have a friend there." She held out her hand to shake Mel's, and the American took it gladly. She wondered briefly if Ainia would grow up to be as beautiful as this woman of mixed races, and she looked at the woman speculatively, wondering about her as she glanced between Carmen and the station owner.

Harold was next, having returned from helping one of the stockmen get his sheep out to new pasturage and checking some of the southern paddocks they were hoping to reuse. He heartily congratulated Mel but moved on quickly, not acknowledging Alinta, and Mel noted that. He moved determinedly to the table where some of the stockmen's wives had set up a little celebration. There was rum in a keg as well as some food. The men packing up the bags of wool rotated out, so they could get a share of rum and a little food before they would be going. The carters were anxious to be on their way, knowing how long a trek it was back to Sydney.

That evening, Mel handed the lead carter a bag with mail for her station that could be sent out from Wilcannia or Menindee, depending on which place the man decided to travel through. The men were leaving early the next day, and a mail carrier would take it from there, much faster than the carter could. He already had a bag of mail from Carmen and Fabiola for Twin Station that would be mailed as well. It would take months for him to make his way back to Sydney with his full carts of wool. There was much more than he had anticipated, and he hadn't had a chance to discuss next year's cartage with the station owner. He had no idea that Fabiola and Carmen didn't intend to use his services next year or that some of the mail he carried contained inquiries to other drayage companies for both Twin Station and the newly formed Lawrence Station.

Carmen watched as the carters left the station, heading east on the track leading into the station. She and Fabiola helped Mel and the new men herd the large flock of now shorn sheep north along the track that was forming there. They stopped that night and shared dinner, the flock well-tended with additional dogs and men, who guarded them in shifts.

"Well, Mel. You got through your first year of sheep herding, establishing your station, and shearing," Carmen saluted her with a pannikin of water.

Mel smiled at her friend, looking at her sitting next to Fabiola on a log they had pulled up to the fire. She glanced at the men, who were already rolled up in their blankets asleep, intending to patrol the flock later in shifts. Then, she looked beyond them to the carts that were in a semi-circle around the chosen camp. Her look finally encompassed her wife and child, and she felt content. "I thank you," she said, returning the salute with her own pannikin, this one containing coffee that had come in with the supplies.

Carmen saw that look towards Alinta and understood it. She wondered if she would ever find someone, and at that moment she noticed Fabiola. She had known that Mel wasn't the companion she was seeking in life but counted her as a true friend. Fabiola had never had a mate, and she wondered if there was a reason behind that. She briefly thought of Harold and immediately dismissed that. His interest was apparent, but something about the weak-willed man repelled her.

Paco had noticed Carmen's repugnance of the man, and he spread the word to their men to keep Harold at bay, if possible. Harold had tried to order the vaqueros around, but they made it clear that they worked for the senora and no other. Occasionally, they would do as Miss Fabiola asked but only out of respect for the senora.

As Carmen and Fabiola headed back towards Twin Station the next day flanked by several vaqueros, Mel and her people were well on their way north to establish this new, raw station she had named Lawrence Station. They smiled, urging their mounts into an impromptu race as Dancer easily outdistanced the Brumby that Fabiola was riding. The two women laughed joyously, well-matched and looking towards the future.

About the Author

K'Anne Meinel is the BEST-SELLING author of LAWYERED, REPRESENTED, SAPPHIC SURFER, DOCTORED, VEIL OF SILENCE, SURVIVORS, VETTED and CAVALCADE as well as several other books including her first, SHIPS which was written in 2003 over the course of two weeks. A gypsy at heart, she has lived in many locations and plans to continue roaming. Videos of several of her books are available on YouTube outlining some of the locations of her books and telling a little bit more…giving the readers insight into her mind as she created these wonderful stories. As of this date she has more than 102 published works including shorts, novellas, and novels. She is an American author born in Milwaukee, Wisconsin and raised in Oconomowoc. Upon early graduation from high school she went to a private college in Milwaukee and then moved to California for seventeen years before returning to the state. Many of her stories have Wisconsin in them as settings for her wonderful, realistic, and detailed backgrounds. Named the lesbian Danielle Steel of her time, K'Anne continues to write interesting stories in a variety of genres in both the lesbian and mainstream fiction categories. Her website is www.kannemeinel.com.

If you have enjoyed **OUTBACK HERITAGE**, I hope you will enjoy
this excerpt from
AN ISLAND BETWEEN US

The war is over, and the boys are coming home. It's time for women everywhere to leave the factories and return to their rightful places...in the kitchen.

Women did their duty and filled many traditionally male jobs while their men were fighting for their country, but now, the men are back and ready to take over. But what if your man didn't return? And what if you found you enjoyed the freedom your job gave you?

Neither Marion Whiting nor Barbara Jenkins loved their jobs in the mill; however, they did the best job they could for their government, and after being widowed by the war, those jobs had become a necessity.

The two women fell in love and moved in together to save on expenses, but they soon discovered life is very different from when they were married to men. After giving up their individual homes in order to buy a place together, they learn that no bank will give them a loan without a responsible male's signature. Since Marion and Barbara no longer have men to 'take care' of them, they decide they will take care of themselves and each other.

Dreams are meant to be pursued, so Marion and Barbara buy an island using the last of their combined money. They want to create a vacation getaway where they can raise their shared family, but they have no idea what it will take to make their dreams on this island a reality.

Will they have to give up their dreams to save their relationship? Will the freedoms they enjoy be thwarted by outside influences? Come along as two women in post-war Maine embark on their dream. "What could possibly go wrong?" you ask...

CHAPTER ONE

As the ferry finally docked, Marion breathed a deep sigh of relief. The trip had been long, too long, and she worried that it would be impossible to make money with the idea they were pursuing. Maybe this had been a wasted trip? It was a wild idea, and she worried that she and Barbara were crazy to even entertain these thoughts. But it felt right, and they had to try. It felt like if they didn't get out of their boring life, they would smother from the sameness of it all. If their lives alone didn't kill them, someone else would. You see, they were a lesbian couple. They'd managed to fool some of the townspeople in the small village outside of Boston where they were escaping from, but some people were suspicious that two young widows living together and not searching for husbands were perhaps more than they appeared. Marion didn't really care, but she worried that Barbara might accidentally be hurt if anyone realized what they were to each other.

As the ferry hit another wave and caused her to sway on her feet, she wondered if she was going to be sick once more. She hoped not. Already, people were staying well away from the seasick woman but thankfully, not Barbara. Barbara held a basin for her time and again, mopped her brow, and even fetched water from the drinking fountain in the corner to soothe her acid-filled stomach. The hours on this ferry had been hell. They hadn't realized how long it would take to get to this corner of Maine. She was also craving a cigarette, having smelled the smoke from the one that was inevitably planted in the corner of Barbara's lips. She knew if she had one puff though, the motion sickness she was suffering would only get worse.

"We're almost there," Barbara said soothingly, her cold hand lovingly caressing the forehead of her sweaty and sick girlfriend. She removed her cigarette with her other hand and flicked the ashes onto the deck of the ship without a thought. Looking at its length, she took one more drag, before flicking it over the rail.

"Sadly, we have to make the return trip," Marion mumbled as she took deep, cleansing breaths—in through her nose and out through her mouth—and hoped she could keep down the water in her stomach. There was nothing else. The last food she had eaten was dinner last night, at least thirteen hours ago. She could only hope that when she touched land again, she would be able to eat. The cool, crisp, and clean air of this part of the world felt good on her face and in her lungs…she could taste the air.

"That's days from now," Barbara reminded her, wondering how someone so steady could succumb to seasickness. The trip hadn't been that bad, and she'd ridden it out with no problem at all, but her petite, effeminate, and fastidious girlfriend had started puking within hours of boarding the ferry. Still, this was the easiest way to get to where they were going.

The rockiness of the ferry began to smooth out as they came into the bay and headed for Franklin. The town was spread out along the mountainside, and for a moment, the dreary fog that had accompanied them all morning lifted, giving them a brief glimpse. Hearing Barbara's intake of breath and feeling the difference in the motion of the ferry, Marion began to get up for a look. The fog closed in again almost instantly, and the rain continued, but she had gotten a glimpse, and that sight had given her hope. For a moment she forgot about her rolling stomach and the long, gruesome trip they had taken. This was for their future, their dream, and she wanted desperately to make it work.

They had taken a few days off from the mill where they worked. This was unprecedented. They'd worked hard during the war and even afterwards when their husbands hadn't come home. Finding each other and feeling an attraction had been a surprise. Acting on that attraction had been something neither had anticipated. Discovering that they could love another human being, another woman, had been a wonderful experience for both.

Pooling their resources and their families, they had come together under one roof. Their sons shared a bedroom, Marion's daughter had her own room, and for anyone who wondered, the two adults shared a bedroom with two double beds for propriety's sake. The fact that only one bed was frequently used was known only by the women since they rose before their sons and daughter and went to bed after them. Their bedroom door was locked when they were inside and only a loud banging on it would have them get up to see which child needed their

mother. Many was the time that Marion or Barbara had rolled on the unused bed to make it look like they didn't share the same bed. So far, their children hadn't caught on, but people in their small town had started whispering. They wondered why two women in the prime of their lives hadn't begun looking for new husbands to replace the ones they had lost in the war. There was an abundance of men, who had come home to take over the jobs the women had been doing in the factories during the war. The independence displayed by these two women was the antithesis of how women in post-war America were expected to behave, so their very lives were being questioned.

As the ferry bumped into the dock of Franklin, Maine, they both breathed a sigh of relief. Gathering their single suitcases and purses, they got in the queue to leave the ferry and get on the dock. Entering the station, both were pleased to be back on solid land. Barbara led the way as Marion was still fighting her nausea, but surely, being on land would help to ease that.

"Excuse me. I'm looking for a Henry Wheeler?" Barbara asked at the ticket office. Her accent had the man looking up at her, immediately identifying her as someone from out of state and not a local.

"Ayuh, that's 'im over there," he said, thumb pointing to the corner where an older man stood, hands in the pockets of his overalls, viewing the crowd. He looked comfortable, rocking back and forth to a tune in his head as he looked about at the throng of passengers getting off the ferry. Some were being greeted by family, and others were making their way through the crush.

"Thank you," she answered politely and led the deep-breathing Marion towards the man.

"Mr. Wheeler?" Barbara asked brightly as they approached.

"Yup, that's me," he answered, looking her over and then glancing at the petite blonde.

Marion knew what he saw. She'd known that her looks were the ticket to her future. They had landed her a good and handsome husband, a fine home, and a future that was assured. Then, World War II had hit and ruined it all for them. Her son and daughter were left without a father, and the small amount of money the government had given her hadn't been enough to survive on. Fortunately, Brian had taken out life insurance. They'd lived on that until she found a job and eventually sold their house. His family hadn't been happy about that, but she felt she didn't need such a big house when the larger family they anticipated would never be born. Today, that face had gone through hell on the trip here and looked pasty. She was not looking her best.

Eventually, after meeting Barbara, they had moved into an apartment together. In theory, they were pooling their funds and saving towards their future...also together. A short, blonde woman, her hair cut short in the current post-war style, Marion had been cute as a button when Brian met her. Worry and having borne children had caused her to put on a few pounds, and now, she was curvy, almost voluptuous...some might, if they were nasty, call her dumpy. She looked tired, worn, and overworked. Mr. Wheeler took that all in as he looked at her before flicking his eyes to the woman next to her.

Barbara was tall, stocky, and could have passed for a man if not for her carefully made-up face.

"Are you Marion Whiting?" he asked, glancing at the blonde to be sure.

"Yes, and this is Barbara Jenkins," she answered, introducing her companion.

He glanced outside at the weather and then looked back at the two women, unsure. "Did you want to go see the land today?"

"It rains a lot here, doesn't it?" Marion smiled as she asked, glancing outside as though to confirm her statement.

He nodded and waited for her to answer his question.

"Do you think it will clear up a little later?"

He looked out again, considering, rubbing his chin. "Ayuh, it could clear up, but then again, it might not."

Marion looked puzzled at this answer. Trying not to lose her cheerful attitude she glanced at Barbara and gave her a grin. "Well, we've been traveling far too many hours without a meal. We'll check into our hotel. Would you like to join us for lunch, Mr. Wheeler?"

He looked surprised that she would make the offer. "No, no, my Martha will have dinner on the table," he told her. "It's a good, long way out there. Maybe we should go tomorrow?"

Considering they only had a couple of days, this limited window of opportunity seemed to be slipping through their fingers. Marion glanced back at Barbara again and saw her chin make a gesture, telling her to go ahead with whatever she meant to say. "I was hoping to see it today," she said firmly. She knew it would be cold, wet, and not an ideal situation, but they couldn't afford not to see it as soon as possible and make up their minds.

Stroking his chin, he considered. "I guess we could go later," he said slowly, thoughtfully.

"That would be wonderful. Could you point us to our hotel? Maybe a diner?"

In his slow, methodical way Mr. Wheeler began to point out the layout of the town. The mist was too thick to see everything he was pointing out, but as he spoke it lifted enough to make out where they needed to go. They watched as he made his way out wearing his rubber Wellingtons, the wetness soon drifting off the point of his hat that matched not only his boots but his knee-length coat, which was open to reveal the overalls. By then, Marion was able to breathe easier. The cool air and solid ground were helping, and they set out for their hotel. Barbara carried their bags while Marion held a large umbrella over them.

"I don't think that was an auspicious beginning," Barbara murmured as they trudged along, not nearly like the long-legged stride their guide had taken. She was pleased to see the color coming back to her girlfriend's pale face, and her chipper attitude hid the nausea she had felt all night long.

"Well, if you wait for spring sunshine in Maine, you might have to wait a while," she quipped with a smile. She too was worried that this dream of theirs was merely an impulse, and she already knew their families would balk at their idea once they heard.

They checked into the town's only hotel and were surprised yet pleased when they were informed there was only one queen-sized bed and they would have to share. They pretended not to mind.

They freshened up and Marion changed her clothes where some of the sick had splashed. She was finally feeling dry and comfortable in her clothes. She washed out her dress to lay it out and let it dry. They went back out into the weather, barely needing their umbrella any longer as the sun had burned off the mist and the rain had gone out to sea. The diner was full of locals who stared at the two women as they ordered. Marion was able to eat, which further calmed her nervous stomach. She was feeling fine as they made their way back to the hotel in time to catch Mr. Wheeler, who was just leaving the lobby.

"Mr. Wheeler?" Marion called as he turned away from them.

He stopped, surprised to be addressed and then smiled slightly upon seeing the two women. "I was just leavin'," he told them in his slow way. He looked at them and their outfits, looking them up and down. Women wearing pants was still a new thing to a lot of people.

"We just finished our lunch and were hoping to find you," she answered sweetly, glancing at Barbara and exchanging a look.

"Ya still want to go out and take a look?" he asked, staring at their outfits.

"We'd love to," she answered, trying to smile but unsure if he was happy with the idea or not.

"Me boat's this way," he pointed down towards the docks, away from the ferry. He clearly didn't approve of women wearing dungarees but turned away quickly.

They followed him and were surprised at the small boat but got in gingerly where he indicated. He started the small motor and headed out of the harbor into the open sea before heading northeast with confidence. Both women held on tightly to the small boat, balancing against the oncoming waves, wondering what they had gotten themselves into.

Barbara worried that Marion would get seasick again and glanced at her repeatedly, but she seemed to be holding her own.

Marion wondered if her full stomach was a mistake, but this smaller boat seemed to ride the waves differently. The water was closer to them, and while they couldn't see as much, it felt better. She looked out as far as she could see from her seat and was pleased to see a patch of sunshine trying to eke out a spot in the overcast above them. The fresh breeze seemed to help her overcome any lingering nausea that might have reared its ugly head.

They saw several islands as Mr. Wheeler motored along, seemingly unaware of anything but his intended destination. The islands looked quiet and unassuming. They were full of lush foliage and tall trees, and the rocks surrounding them made some of them appear menacing. There was no sign of life. Marion pointed out different trees, but Barbara looked out at the water, wondering how far out they were going. Finally, Mr. Wheeler turned towards almost open sea, and they spotted an island. It didn't look like much as he followed along its rocky coastline. The kelp along the stony shore wasn't promising. In fact, it looked downright foreboding. A narrow opening turned into a cove, which widened out into about a half-mile-long lagoon and looked promising. He drove the smaller boat right up onto the "sand," which was more rock than sand. Fortunately, this island's shores didn't have the large boulders of the other islands or those shores that the ocean constantly pounded on.

"This is 'er," he spoke for the first time since they had left Franklin and pointed with his thumb behind him from where he was tying off the small craft.

Both women carefully got out of the boat and looked about. The small cove would be perfect for landing a craft such as the one Mr. Wheeler owned but they knew they would need a bigger one if they were to make this project work. Barbara looked at Marion, wondering at her thoughts. Marion was looking avidly about, expanding and making plans from her vague ideas now that she was seeing the island.

"Well, let's look around, shall we?" Barbara asked, trying to sound enthusiastic. Marion smiled as she eagerly began the walk up from the small beach despite there being no path.

"Someone once had a shack up dere on the bluff," Mr. Wheeler offered, not too enthusiastic about traipsing off into the woods where the women had headed. Still, he had been surprised to get their letter inquiring about his ad, which had read:

'Small island on the Canada/United States border. Excellent timber. Whimsical Island. Serious inquiries via P.O. Box 102, Franklin, Maine.'

He was certain he was wasting his time with these two women. Still, they *had* traveled all the way from Massachusetts.

Barbara had been the one to find the ad in the newspaper and show it to Marion. Marion hadn't even thought about it more than an hour before she wrote the *serious inquiry* letter to Mr. Wheeler. "Remember how camp seemed to be the best place there was when you were a child?" she enthused as she made plans for an island she had never even seen.

"Marion, I didn't go to the same camps you did," Barbara pointed out. They hadn't been in the same social classes and *camp* was not an option for her. The one year Barbara had been able to go to camp hadn't endeared her to the idea in the same way it obviously was taking hold of Marion.

"Do you not want me to send the letter?" Marion had asked, slightly hurt and yet willing to do whatever Barbara wanted.

"No, inquire away," she encouraged her, wondering if they could get out of the mill jobs where they weren't wanted now that the boys were back from the war. They had been just two of the very few women who clung tenaciously to the few jobs left available once the men returned. They were resented because they were female. Even more so because they were widows and survivor's guilt riddled some of the men, knowing they had survived and not these women's husbands. They were constant reminders that men had died, their friends had died, and they had not. These women had given their all…and then some.

They both discussed the possibility that they could move out of the village and far away from Boston, their families, their husband's families, and the disapproving friends, acquaintances, and even strangers, who suspected the true nature of their relationship. It was time to start over, and this ad seemed like a godsend.

Mr. Wheeler's letter hadn't been welcoming, but it hadn't been discouraging either. He had invited them up to Franklin to view the island and consider its purchase. Both women wondered if anyone in post-war America had the money to buy an island, much less visit one, and they knew it might be the most foolish venture either could consider. Once they were able to arrange the time off from work, they had penned another letter, accepting his invitation and letting him know the date of their arrival.

Mr. Wheeler watched as the women made their way away from the boat and up into the trees. They couldn't get lost. The island was only half a mile or so across and four miles long from tip to tip. He sat back down and pulled out a pipe.

Marion was pointing out the beauties they were seeing, almost as though Barbara couldn't see them for herself. There were great stone cliffs along one edge of the non-existent trail they were making. Great maple trees—hundreds of years old, thick and luxurious, and about to leaf-out in the early spring growth—were mixed with tall pines and other trees. They found other smaller beaches, one with odd shells that were crushed along the rocky shore. They heard the gulls, and other strange birds made their presence known. A majestic Great Blue Heron took wing from a meadow as they explored. The sun came out and dried up their path, making it a hike and a hot walk, which they both welcomed. They loosened their button-up jackets as they trekked along.

"What's that?" Barbara pointed, startled as a brown-furred animal slithered away through last year's growth.

"I think that was a mink," Marion answered, amused at her usually brave girlfriend's fright.

It was a good thing they were here so early in the spring after the winter snows had melted; the undergrowth would have been impossible to walk through otherwise. They found a game trail that had obviously been made by deer and followed it as it made the going easier.

"Gosh, Barbara," Marion's voice trembled with emotion, "how could anything be so beautiful and uninhabited?" Used to the noise of the big city, even in their small village, they both marveled at the quiet and the fact that no one was about.

They spent quite a bit of time roaming the island. Then realizing that Mr. Wheeler might be alarmed that they had become lost, they began to make their way back, hoping to find the large cove without too much trouble. They slid down a few steep slopes in their attempt to make a trail, abandoning the animal trail in order to find a straighter route to the cove. There was lots of moss on the trees, and Marion warned Barbara never to believe that adage that moss only grew on one side of the trees. "It'll grow wherever it can," she informed the city girl.

"To think these views are going to waste and we're stuck looking into the apartments across the way from ours," Barbara said as she took in the deep woods and ocean surrounding them as they made their way back to the boat.

They were both relieved to see Mr. Wheeler patiently waiting for them, smoking a pipe as he sat in the bow of his boat.

"Ya seen 'nough?" he asked, cordially. He didn't seem perturbed that they had kept him waiting for hours as they explored the island.

Both women nodded enthusiastically. They helped to push the boat off the small pebble spit, less sand than they had originally thought. They both watched as the old man expertly started his motor and they puttered out of the protective cove. The feel of the open water was almost immediate beyond the trees that marked the entrance, the deeper water a little rougher but nothing like the ferry, which had a deeper draft and bucked the waves differently. They both stared at the receding island thoughtfully. Each of them looked forward to discussing it later when they were alone. They didn't want to talk in front of the old man, and the ever-present winds blowing their hair into their faces made it difficult to be heard.

"Thank you so much for the ride, Mr. Wheeler," Barbara said politely as he pulled his boat onto the shore in Franklin.

"Yes, thank you. We will let you know what we decide," Marion told him as they both got out of the boat.

He nodded cordially but was thinking to himself that he had wasted his entire afternoon on two *women*. What in the world could they have been thinking? He tied off his boat and made his way into the small town, moving away from them and not saying a word.

"Well, are you hungry again, or should we return to the hotel and discuss what we saw?" Marion asked, wondering how Barbara's stomach was feeling. She knew her own had recovered sufficiently that she was starving.

"I could eat," she began slowly, already lost in thought over the island. She was burgeoning with ideas and wondered if they could afford to act on them all.

They didn't talk about the island as they ate at the diner again. The locals were listening in avidly. It was so obvious it was almost amusing. They understood and smiled in a friendly manner at the eavesdroppers as they ate their meals.

"What do you think?" Marion asked as soon as they were in the safety of their hotel room.

"I liked it," Barbara began cautiously, her eyes sparkling with the excitement she was feeling. She had felt so alive on that island, and she hadn't felt like that in what seemed like forever. Then she rethought that. She felt alive in Marion's arms, but it was so different from what *this* idea and concept felt like.

"We could build a cabin…or ten and rent them out," Marion put in, her own enthusiasm trickling out. She wasn't fooled by Barbara's quiet demeanor. She saw the sparkle in her eyes, and it was exciting.

"Do you think we should?" she asked, again sounding cautious.

"I think God puts things in your path for a reason. We both hate our lives in the mill and are slowly dying inside. I felt as though my soul got aired out on that island today. I'd like to go back and poke around. Do you think Mr. Wheeler would lend us his boat?"

Barbara immediately shook her head. "I bet we can rent one somewhere."

"You think they would rent to two women?" Merion mused.

She had to admit the blonde had a point. It was frustrating that two competent women were not allowed to do things simply because of their sex. Things had changed since before the war. Still, they had to conform a bit for society. "I want to go back," Barbara admitted.

"You think two people could make a living on an island like that?"

"I wondered that too. There's that one meadow, and we could plant an orchard and a garden, but that wouldn't really bring in that much money," she mused, thinking practically. "What about the initial price of the island?"

"No bank is going to lend a woman money without a man to co-sign," Marion pointed out, reminding her what had happened before and paraphrasing what they had been told.

Barbara nodded. They'd already known that. Even when Marion was selling her house, they had come up against the condescension that a woman alone couldn't possibly understand the intricacies involved in such a complicated financial transaction. "There's the money from the sale of my house," she mentioned, as though they both hadn't already thought of that.

"And my house as well as the life insurance policies."

"Shouldn't we save something in case something goes wrong?"

"We could always go back and work at the mill," Marion pointed out, although the thought of failure depressed them both, much less the thought of working at the mill for the rest of their lives. "Brian always said, 'Nothing ventured, nothing gained.'"

Barbara nodded, a little jealous of the man in her girlfriend's past life. Still, he was gone, killed in the war like her own husband, and nothing was going to bring them back. "Bob had the same kind of saying, but it was me that managed to get us that house," she said nostalgically, missing the house that had been their home but not the man. She didn't regret getting rid of the house to take up housekeeping with this woman she had come to love so much. Their love had surprised both women with its intensity and even the fact that two women could be in love with each other. After selling their homes, they ended up living in an apartment. They hadn't realized they couldn't get another mortgage without a man signing the financial paperwork with them. Neither one would think of bothering their male relatives with such a matter. Most of their extended family felt they were a little too independent raising their three children together. What they should have done was sold one of the houses and moved in together, but they had thought they could buy another house together...until the banks had told them no.

"So, we buy the island outright and build from the ground up?"

Barbara nodded slowly, worrying about the money and their finances. They had enough between them to buy the island and build a small house on it, but the thought of what else they would need scared her. It meant giving up a safety net that they just might need later.

"We'll need a boat, some sort of dock, as well as a million other things we haven't even thought of." Marion started ticking off things on her fingers.

"The children will have to start correspondence school."

"The children are going to love this adventure," the petite blonde pointed out, knowing their children hadn't been happy to give up their homes and their yards to live in a much smaller apartment.

They discussed a lot of things, agreeing on almost everything before they headed to bed. They were tired from the trip on the ferry, exploring the island, and the fresh air. Their initial attempts to make love proved that the bed had squeaky springs, and not wishing to be discovered, they decided to hold off until they had more privacy.

TO BE CONTINUED…

~End sample chapter of AN ISLAND BETWEEN US~
For more go to www.Shadoepublishing.com to purchase the complete book or for many other delightful offerings

~ Because a publisher should stand behind their authors~

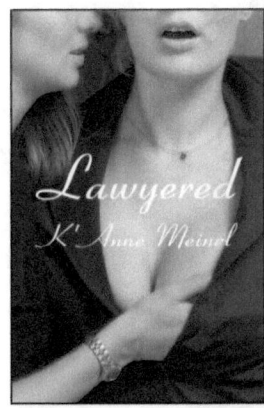
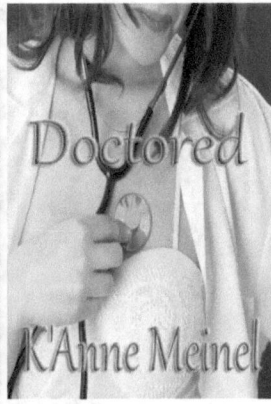

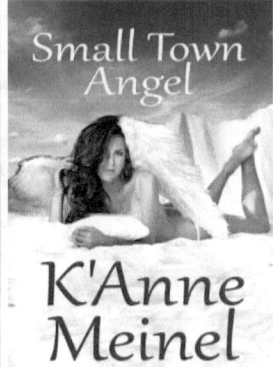

~ Because a publisher should stand behind their authors~

What do you do when you meet someone who changes everything you know about love and passion?

Paige Harlow is a good girl. She's always known where she was going in life: top grades, an ivy league school, a medical degree, regular church attendance, and a happy marriage to a man. Falling in love with her gorgeous roommate and best friend Alyssa Torres is no small crisis. Alyssa is chasing demons of her own, a medical condition that makes her an outcast and a family dysfunctional to the point of disintegration make her a questionable choice for any stable relationship. But Paige's heart is no longer her own. She must now battle the prejudices of her family, friends, and church and come to peace with her new sexuality before she can hope to win the affections of the woman of her dreams. But will love be enough?

~ Because a publisher should stand behind their authors~

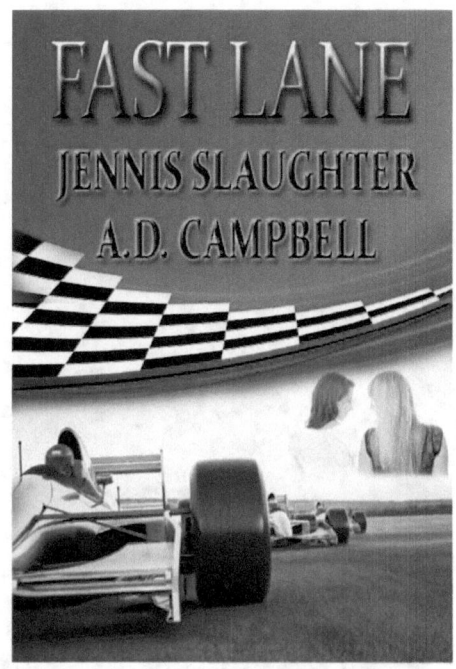

In the male dominated sport of Formula 1 racing, Samantha 'Sam' Dupree is struggling to make her mark against the boys. She hears about a driver who is making a name for herself in NASCAR and goes to check her out. Little does she know that she's in for the race of her heart.

Addison McCloud wants nothing more than to drive. She doesn't care about fame or fortune; she just wants to be fast enough to get herself and her family away from her abusive father. Meeting Sam, changes her world and revs her life into overdrive.

When the two women meet, sparks flies like the race cars that they drive, Will they be able to steer their relationship into something more and win the race, or will their families make them crash and burn. The boys of Formula 1 are going to learn that Southern girls are a force to be reckoned with.

~ *Because a publisher should stand behind their authors~*

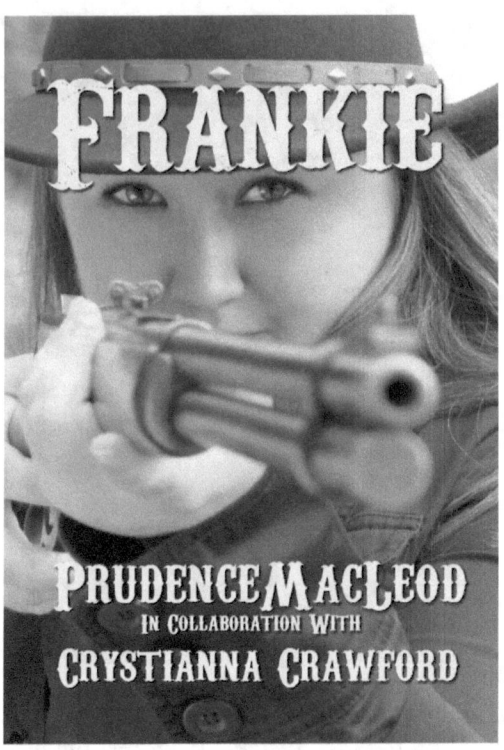

Carrie flees from the demons of her present, trying to protect the ones she loves.

Frankie hides from the demons of her past, and the memory of loved ones she failed to protect.

A modern day princess thrown to the wolves, Carrie's only hope is the rancher who had spent the better part of a decade in self imposed, near total, isolation. Frankie's history of losing those she tries to save haunts her, but this madman threatens her home, her livestock, her sanctuary. She knows she can't do it alone, has she still got enough support from her oldest friends?

www.shadoepublishing.com

Amelia Gittens had the credit of being the first and only woman thus far in the United States military of being a sniper in combat, made possible by being in the Military Police unit of the crack 10th Mountain Infantry Division. After retirement she joins the City of New York Police Department, and suddenly finds herself involved in a suspect shooting incident which soon encroaches upon her entire life. In order to protect her therapist who has been targeted as a revenge killing, Amelia takes on the responsibility as if she was still in the Army, treating it as a tactical maneuver.

~ Because a publisher should stand behind their authors~

When U.S. Marine Dakota McKnight returned home from her third tour in Operation Iraqi Freedom, she carried more baggage than the gear and dress blues she had deployed with. A vicious rocket-propelled grenade attack on her base left her best friend dead and Dakota physically and emotionally wounded. The marine who once carried herself with purpose and confidence, has returned broken and haunted by the horrors of war. When she returns to the civilian world, life is not easy, but with the help of her therapist, Janie, she is barely managing to hold her life together...then she meets Beth.

Beth Kendrick is an American history college professor. She is as straight-laced as they come, until Dakota enters her life, that is. Will her children understand what she is going through? Will she take a chance on the broken marine or decide to wait for the perfect someone to come along?

Time is on your side, they say, unless there is a dark, sinister evil at work. Is their love strong enough to hold these two people together? Will the love of a good woman help Dakota find the path to recovery? Or is she doomed to a life of inner turmoil and destruction that knows no end?

www.shadoepublishing.com

If you have enjoyed this book and the others listed here Shadoe Publishing, LLC is always looking for first, second, or third time authors. Please check out our website @ www.shadoepublishing.com For information or to contact us @ shadoepublishing@gmail.com.

We may be able to help you bring your dreams of becoming a published author to life.

www.ingramcontent.com/pod-product-compliance
Lightning Source LLC
Chambersburg PA
CBHW050937120626
46552CB00001B/255